A New Start

Morris Fenris

A New Start

Table of Contents

Chapter 1

Maggie moved the box to one side of the room and then to the other. She sighed a long, tired sigh and moved it back again; then she flopped down onto the long, low sofa and snuggled into its soft, feather seats. She was pleased with her purchase which replaced the old, leather 'man' sofa. This was much more her. That's what it was all about now, her and no-one else.

Staring at the ceiling, she reflected on the last twenty-five years of her life. Where had they gone? What happened to her over the years? She'd lost herself, that's what happened. She'd lost her independence, lost it to a selfish, cheating man. She wouldn't even call him husband, although technically, till the divorce came through, that's what he was. "I can't believe him!" she said out loud to no one in the room. Even though she thought she was over Leonard, his betrayal still hurt her. It was difficult to get over twenty five years of marriage. Tears filled her eyes and began to stream down her cheeks. Why did she cry? Not for him, surely! She wasn't sure exactly what it was she cried for; it could be the perfect life she had created for herself. She had had that picture perfect family, a wonderful man, a beautiful daughter, and a comfortable lifestyle. Then one day it had all come crashing down around her.

"He's not good for you Maggie," her mother's words rang in her head as if she'd just heard them yesterday. She didn't know how many times she had wished she'd listened to her mother. Of course, she'd attributed her mother's dislike for him to the fact he was her first serious boyfriend. After dedicating herself to studying and becoming a lawyer, she had felt proud of herself for finally starting a relationship.

Her friends had made it hard enough with all their teasing throughout the years since high school. They'd constantly tried to set her up with their friends or cousins, insisting they were perfect for her and she should focus more on life rather than her career.

Maggie gave a little smirk at the memory. They had been so sure they were right, and maybe they had been, but now no one would ever know.

Reminiscing had a way of taking over Maggie's mind and now that she'd started the flow of memories, they just kept coming.

She remembered the day that Leonard Faulkner had joined the law firm she worked at. He was so suave, so attentive, he had captured the eye of every girl there. Maggie couldn't help but smile as she thought back to the incessant pleasantries and jokes she and Leonard had shared. They had seemed to have so much in common and got along so well.

When Leonard had asked her to marry him eight months into their relationship, Maggie hadn't even thought twice. She had been in love, so enamored with him and who they were together, she couldn't imagine her life anywhere else than at his side.

Maggie pulled one of the many unpacked boxes closer and opened it up. A pink photo album stared up at her. Its front was slightly faded and the ribbon below the photo was frayed at the edges, but it brought happy tears instead of sad ones.

Maggie picked the album up gently and ran her fingers over the black and white ultrasound photo. Some had told her that Gillian had been the end of her life, but in a way, she had been the beginning of a new one.

It had been right around the time that Maggie became pregnant that Leonard had decided he was meant for politics instead of law. It had seemed only right that she give up her career and help Leonard to progress on his chosen path.

She had always planned to go back to the law firm, it just hadn't worked out.

As she flipped through the baby pictures in the album she thought about Gillian's birth. Although Maggie loved her daughter more than life itself. She had never really been into all the maternal things, especially the giving birth part.

"Goodness that was the worst," she said softly to herself. She glanced around the empty apartment. She didn't know when she had started talking to an empty room, but it felt better than not saying anything at all.

Pregnancy had been a challenge, but birth had taken the cake for difficulty. How great it would have been to be put to sleep till the whole birth was over.

Maggie stopped at a photo of herself holding baby Gillian.

Two months and fourteen days was written underneath the space below the photo. Maggie stared at the happy young woman holding the tiny baby. She looked vibrant, excited about life, and proud of the achievement she held in her arms.

If only Maggie could turn back the clock, go back to those days. With a sigh she set the photo album back into the box. She wasn't ready to do this today. Maybe the boxes could wait a while longer.

It was hard for her to find the motivation for projects like this, projects that reminded her of a painful past. Her eyes wandered to the entrance of the apartment where her running shoes sat. She loved running. The fact that she was fifty didn't keep her cooped up in the house. In fact, she kept herself in quite good shape. Running had always been her preferred exercise. A run sounded nice right about now. The idea of a cool breeze hitting her face as her heels pounded the sidewalk got her up out of her sitting position quicker than anything could have.

These boxes could wait. After all, they had waited six weeks. What was another day? This wasn't a day to sit inside her lonely apartment and cry about the things she'd lost. A nice long run outdoors would be good therapy.

Her fingers moved excitedly to tie her shoelaces when lightning flashed across the wall and a clap of thunder stopped her. She padded across the floor and drew back the curtain. With a groan she let the delicate fabric fall back into place just as the sound of soft raindrops on the roof began. Was this her life from now on? Would nothing ever go right again? With a frustrated grumble she went back to her couch and plopped down. It looked like the boxes were going to be her project for today after all.

The shrill tone of the house phone filled the air and broke her train of thought. Reaching across the small art deco table, Maggie hurried to answer it.

"Hello?" she said into the phone.

"Hi, Mom!" It was good to hear her daughter's voice, even though it was through the phone. It made the apartment feel less lonely.

"What are you doing tomorrow, Mom?"

"I barely know what I'm doing today," Maggie sighed, looking out the window at the rain that was still pouring down in sheets. "I was going to go for a run, till the storm started."

"Well," Gillian voice paused for a moment, "How about you come and help me at the orphanage tomorrow?"

"With the children?" Maggie wasn't sure she was up for a day with children. While Gillian seemed to love her work at the orphanage, and Maggie fully supported her, it wasn't exactly her preferred line of work.

"Yes, with the children, Mom, it'll be fun. Remember when I was a kid? We had fun."

A rush of memories as Gillian when she was a little girl filled Maggie's mind. She had been one of the bright spots of her life.

"Well, that was a little different. You were my child," Maggie stated doubtfully.

"Mom, these kids are the sweetest you'll ever meet. You just have to see their little faces to fall in love with them."

"Well, if they're that sweet, how come they're still in the orphanage?" Maggie didn't expect her daughter to completely understand her sense of humor, but if someone would at least appreciate it, it would be Gillian.

"Mom, you're just terrible!" Gillian's annoyed voice sounded a little louder in the phone now.

"Look, why don't you just give it a chance? You haven't been over since you and dad separated, and I think it would be good for you to get out and about.

"I'm taking some of the younger kids to see Santa and I could use the extra hands," she added.

There was silence on the line as Maggie considered the offer.

Maybe it wouldn't be a bad idea to get out of the apartment.

"Okay, I'll come," Maggie finally said with a sigh. She was sure she most likely wouldn't be having much fun but visiting with her daughter could never be bad. She hadn't realized how much she missed Gillian until she had moved out. There were so many things Maggie wished she could change about their relationship, but she had no idea where to start, so instead, she tried to do what she could with the rare time they spent together these days.

"Thanks Mom. I really appreciate it. Can you be here by eleven?"

"Yes, I'll be there by eleven." Maggie wanted to sound excited, but she just couldn't find it in herself. Somehow, she'd lost her enthusiasm for new adventure a long time ago.

"Okay, see you then," Gillian remained on the line even after she'd said goodbye.

Maggie knew they were both waiting for something. She wanted to tell her daughter she loved her, thank her for calling, that she couldn't wait for the next day. But even as the words formed themselves in her mind, they evaporated.

"Okay, bye," she said, then cut the line.

It seemed that it was too late to change her relationship with Gillian, no matter how much she wanted to.

Maggie picked up a black pen and wrote 'visit orphanage' in the next-day activity box on her calendar. It wasn't as if the calendar was full, it was just a habit Maggie had created over the years, and one that she wasn't quite ready to give up.

Turning back to the awaiting boxes, she tried to keep her mind distracted with the next day's visit. By the evening she found herself actually looking forward to it.

Chapter 2

Gillian stared down at the phone in her hand. Every call ended the same. She remembered when she was a kid and would be at a friend's house and hear them saying goodbye to their parents. She had always wanted that from her mom. The little, "I love you" at the end of the call, or "I miss you," but it never came.

She didn't necessarily blame her mother. She knew it was hard for her to express her feelings, especially after everything she had been through.

Gillian shook her head slightly as her father popped into mind, another parent who had disappointed her. She didn't hate either of her parents. She loved them more than they could imagine, she just wasn't sure exactly how she was supposed to fit into their lives.

"What did she say?" her friend Lorna asked as she walked into the room.

"Oh, she's gonna come. I just hope she has a little fun," Gillian said with a shrug.

"It won't be your fault if she doesn't," Lorna said cheerily, patting Gillian on the shoulder encouragingly.

Gillian managed a little smile. Lorna was always the positive one, pulling people away from their negative thoughts. There was nothing better than having a friend to work with at the orphanage. Lorna had started after Gillian and while Gillian trained her, they had become best friends.

"I'm going to see if the children have finished washing up, or whether we have a flooded kitchen," Lorna said. "Oh, I almost forgot, I need to check the groceries and send in an order for more today," she added. Lorna rushed out of the office towards what Gillian was sure was a mountain of chores to do. While Lorna shared her responsibilities with several others, it was still a lot of work.

As manager of the orphanage, Gillian wasn't directly

responsible for the kids, but that didn't mean that she didn't pull her weight too. She was often the one to cover shifts or to take the children out on special activities when she had time.

As she moved to go help Lorna, the small black and white photograph pinned to the wall beside the doorway caught her eye. It was of the original Tungsten House. Underneath the fading picture it read, *Tungsten Orphanage, 1834.* Gillian liked to think that the Tungsten sisters who had started the orphanage would be proud that they now could accommodate twenty-three children and were finding new homes for orphans all the time.

"Need any help?" Gillian asked, poking her head through the kitchen doorway. It appeared as if Lorna were directing a symphony of little children ranging from four years old all the way up to fifteen in the cleaning and washing of the kitchen.

"I think we've got it covered," Lorna said with a laugh.

Gillian observed them for a few more minutes. The children laughed and played as they helped out. Gillian smiled, she had always had a lot of trepidation about having a family when she was young due to her parent's relationship but the children at the orphanage brought her true joy.

When the opportunity to work at the orphanage had opened up, she had accepted it as a challenge to see how capable she was of being in charge of children.

It hadn't taken her long to fall in love with both the work and the children. While she was one of the main advocates for finding them their forever homes, she was still sad to see any of them go.

After being doubly reassured that everything was handled, she headed down the halls towards the office in the back. The appointment papers for Santa needed to be filed and if she didn't do it, they'd most likely be forgotten about.

The office was small, but cozy; it had two desks, with computers and two filing cabinets. Ideally, they would have one large office instead of one office in the front and one at the back of the orphanage, but they had to work with the rooms they had.

"A penny for your thoughts?" A deep male voice made Gillian jump.

She turned to find Kevin leaning nonchalantly against the doorframe.

"You scared me half to death!" Gillian scolded, unable to keep a smile from her face.

"That's what boyfriends are for, aren't they?" Kevin said with a chuckle.

"No it is not," she exclaimed, swatting him playfully with a hand full of paperwork. Gillian joined in with his contagious chuckle.

"What are you doing? Can I help?" Kevin moved to her side and gave her a quick kiss, before beginning to shuffle through the papers on the desk.

"I'm looking for the contract with Santa Claus for tomorrow," Gillian explained.

Kevin began to meticulously look at each of the papers individually. That was one thing Gillian adored about Kevin. He was always willing to help her with her work, whether that be filing papers, peeling potatoes, or driving kids across town.

Of course, it was expected that he be interested in this type of work, seeing as his father was the patron of the orphanage. It had taken Gillian some time to see that Kevin was truly here for the children and not just to pursue her.

"Here it is!" Kevin held up the missing contract with a beaming smile. "Thanks," Gillian said reaching for the paper.

Kevin held it above his head and smiled mischievously as Gillian reached for it. He put his free arm around her and pulled her into a hug while placing the paper safely on the desk.

"Now that that's out of the way, there was actually something I wanted to talk to you about," he said in a serious tone.

"And what might that be?" Gillian asked skeptically. She was pretty sure she already had an idea of what it was.

"When are you going to tell your mother about me?" Kevin said, holding her in a sort of half embrace.

11

"Kevin, you know I will when the right opportunity presents itself," Gillian said softly. It wasn't that she hadn't wanted to tell her mother, and it certainly wasn't that she was ashamed or embarrassed about her relationship with Kevin. She just wasn't sure how to approach the subject.

Her mother had always warned her about getting married too young, before she had a solid career or had done everything she wanted to in life. And to her mother, having a boyfriend was as good as getting married.

It was a discussion Gillian knew she needed to have but she wasn't looking forward to it. There were so many things her mother didn't know about her and if she disclosed one of them it seemed as if the rest would come tumbling out behind it.

"You've been saying that for the past five months." Kevin said sternly. "How on earth can I propose to you if you won't even tell your mother about us?"

"There's just so much my mother and I-," Gillian stopped, suddenly realizing what Kevin had said. She stared into his earnest blue eyes. "Sorry-," she stammered. "Sorry-, what did you say?"

Kevin released her and put his hand into his pocket, bringing out a little blue velvet box. He held out the box to her. "Would you please tell your mother, so I can ask you to be my wife?" He opened the box, showing a beautiful platinum ring adorned with a crown of diamonds, flanked on either side by an emerald.

Gillian stared at the dazzling stones as the light bounced off them.

"Kevin? I never expected. I mean, you never said. You..." She was so stunned, she couldn't even string a sentence together.

Kevin took the ring out of the box and lifted Gillian's left hand. "Does that mean yes?" He hovered the ring over her hand, his eyes sparkling mischievously.

"Yes," Gillian giggled, tears filling her eyes.

Kevin laughed as he placed the ring on her finger, "You had me worried there for a second," he said with a relieved smile.

It was a perfect fit. Leave it to Kevin to pay attention to the little details, one of the many reasons she had fallen in love with him.

Gillian had never even considered that Kevin had marriage on his mind. While it seemed a little early since they had only been together six months, Gillian felt like it was right.

They gazed at each other for a moment, enjoying the glow they felt. While Gillian knew some girls would have liked to have been proposed to in a restaurant or some other romantic place, she couldn't have imagined a better place to receive the delicate ring that now embraced her finger.

The sudden noise of the office door flying open made them both jump a little.

Lorna stood in the doorway, her dark brown hair looking wild in a controlled way that was only possible for Lorna.

"There you are Gillian, I was wondering if…" She paused at the sight of Kevin.

"Hey Kevin, I didn't know you were coming over today," she said slowly. She looked from one to the other with sudden realization that she had barged in on a private moment.

"Oops, ummm…," she said uncomfortably.

Neither Gillian nor Kevin moved for several seconds. Gillian wasn't sure if Kevin was okay with her making their engagement public. After all they hadn't had time to discuss it before being discovered.

"Are you guys OK? You're acting weird," Lorna accused with a funny smile, as if she wasn't sure what to think of the situation.

Without taking his eyes from Gillian, Kevin raised her left hand to show Lorna the ring.

Gillian giggled, it looked like Kevin was ready to shout it from the rooftops. She just hoped he could keep his excitement hidden long enough for her to let her mother in on the secret.

Lorna's eyes widened and she rushed across the small office

to fling her arms around them both. "Oh, you guys! I'm so happy for you!" Releasing her grip, she rushed back to the door way, stuck her head out of the office and shouted out to anyone who could hear, "Everyone, Gillian and Kevin are getting married!"

It didn't take long for children and staff to start appearing at the doorway of the small office with knowing grins on their faces. Everyone knew about Gillian and Kevin's relationship and from the reactions they were getting, Gillian was pretty sure no one objected to the recent development in their relationship.

More and more people crowded in the small office offering congratulations and wanting to see the ring, asking when the big day would be. Gillian and Kevin took turns telling people that they had only just been engaged and would let them know as soon as they knew more. While Gillian wasn't usually one to enjoy attention, the excitement was contagious. After about half an hour, the children returned to their daily routine. The adults finally tired of asking questions and congratulations and returned to work, leaving Lorna, Kevin and Gillian alone in the office once more.

"Well," Lorna began. "Who's going to tell your mother? You do know, Kevin, that she will most likely run a dozen background checks on you and try to convince Gillian to run." Lorna warned Kevin.

"I don't care, Lorna," Kevin assured her taking Gillian's hands in his and kissing them softly. "Just so long as nothing stops me from making this beautiful lady my wife."

"Nothing will as long as I can help it," Gillian reassured with a laugh before giving Kevin another hug. She was so happy and giddy she just didn't know what to do with herself. Even the daunting task of bringing her mother in on things couldn't get her spirits down today. She smiled up at Kevin. Somehow, her mother would come around and come to love Kevin as much as she did.

Chapter 3

Maggie set the last photograph above her fireplace. Now everything she needed was finally organized and put away. Just like her life would be from now on. No more rushing here and there, trying to organize dinner parties at short notice, making travel plans without having all the information or just making sure no one was saying anything about Leonard that they shouldn't. That was all behind her.

She looked at her neat and orderly living room. It finally looked like someone lived there instead of like a storage room. The last six weeks had been a blur, but it felt good to have things set up and organized. Maybe she would have Gillian over or maybe she would meet some friends.

For a moment, she had the idea of having Gillian's orphanage children come over for a snack or something, but she banished the idea as soon as it appeared. Children would make a mess of the place. It wouldn't be their fault, but Maggie was past those days.

Maggie wondered for a moment if Gillian would ever have children. Then she would definitely have them over to her apartment. Some of Maggie's fondest memories were at her grandmother's house, and she had always vowed to be a good grandmother someday.

"She'd have to find a serious relationship for that though," Maggie said thoughtfully to herself.

Maggie wasn't sure where Gillian had gotten her lack of commitment from, but she certainly hadn't been able to find a man who she could stick with for long. It wasn't for lack of trying, Gillian had gone on more dates than Maggie could remember.

There was the young man from the deli. He had always gotten so tongue tied when Gillian entered the store; it took him six months to get around to asking her out. Maggie was sure Gillian only agreed out of sympathy. She must have liked something about him though, because they dated for about three months. Maggie remembered how when they broke up Gillian had insisted they find somewhere else to have lunch just to avoid him.

There was the doctor on the other hand who was really cute. Maggie had actually had high hopes for him but once she got to know him a bit, she realized she was wrong. He thought he was what every woman wanted, and that he could do no wrong. No wonder Gillian blew him off after only a handful of dates. *There are worse things than not having a relationship,* Maggie thought. *She could have gotten stuck with some rich disrespecting man.*

Thank goodness Gillian had good senses to send the entitled men packing after a single date and sometimes with even less.

Maggie gave a proud smile as she thought of all the times she had seen Gillian stand up for herself. Maggie recognized that she hadn't been the best mother in the world, but at least Gillian had turned out okay.

"*What to do now?*" Maggie thought to herself. Maybe a nice glass of wine and then she would have a look at her next article for the magazine.

Taking up writing as a career had been a big change and it was often stressful, but she enjoyed it in a way.

Being worried about deadlines and bringing in the income to support herself was a liberty that she had forgotten. She glanced at the clock. It was getting late, and maybe she would forgo the article and make it an early night. She wanted to have plenty of rest for her day tomorrow.

As she prepared for bed she thought of all the things she was going to do to repair not only her relationship with her daughter but her life.

She felt a certain excitement but it was mixed with sadness. At one time, she had imagined growing old at Leonard's side, doing all the things they had talked about doing one day. She had thought they would finally take that cruise to Europe and visit Hawaii.

There were days she still missed those dreams, and missed

Leonard. You couldn't just give your life to someone for twenty-five years and then not care about them at all over night.

Deep down, Maggie did hope that Leonard would find happiness and she also hoped that one day she'd be able to forgive him for what he'd done.

With a sad smile, Maggie let herself drift off to sleep.

The alarm pulled Maggie harshly from her sleep. Maggie struggled with the phone, searching for the right button to silence the blaring noise. There were some days she wondered how she had ever let Gillian convince her to buy a smart phone. The old button ones were so much easier to use.

She sighed as she looked at the time. She had plenty of time to get ready.

In her excitement to see her daughter and show her that everything was fine in her life, Maggie took a little extra thought with every little thing she prepared. She combed her hair a little longer than usual and tried on several outfits before she decided on one she thought was appropriate.

Of course she wanted Gillian to have a relationship with Leonard, despite what he had done to their family. After all, he was Gillian's father. Whether he had been a good father or not was not up to Maggie to judge, but up to Gillian.

Maggie sighed as she stared into the mirror, finally ready. She looked so old, so tired. She missed being young and beautiful and ready for life's adventure.

She almost felt guilty about choosing what she would do today. She wasn't supposed to be a single woman looking for ways to entertain herself. She was supposed to be happily married with Leonard in some beach house somewhere.

She shook her head sadly. These thoughts came so often now, they were becoming repetitive. She scolded herself for thinking on it so often.

Leonard had chosen to go off with someone else, someone younger and more beautiful than she would ever be again. That

17

young woman, Maggie was sure, was just out to get his money and his gifts, nothing more. After all, no one would stick by Leonard the way she had, would they?

The thought of Leonard off with another woman still disgusted Maggie as much as the day she had found out.

She remembered how betrayed she'd felt, how utterly hopeless and devastated she had been. Even now, there were days she just felt numb, as if she couldn't experience rage or happiness or any other emotion. She hated this feeling almost worse than the feelings of guilt and despair.

Her therapist had insisted it wasn't her fault, but Maggie couldn't help but wonder, could she have done something differently to create a better outcome for their marriage?

And then still other days she knew in her heart that it was all Leonard's fault. She had done everything right, hadn't she?

With an aggravated huff, she walked to the door, looking back over her tidy apartment. Her eyes swept the apartment searching for anything she had missed. She didn't want to be late meeting Gillian. After all this was a fresh start for them too.

While Maggie had determined not to talk badly to Gillian about her father, she was also determined to show that she was fine without him, even if that wasn't completely true.

With a steady set to her jaw, she hurried to the awaiting taxi. Today was going to be a good day, she was sure of it.

Chapter 4

"Mom, what on earth are you wearing?" Gillian asked when Maggie entered the office.

"What's wrong?" Maggie asked. "I'll have you know this is a Ralph Lauren jacket," Maggie scolded indignantly.

Gillian gave a patient smile. "You know we are just taking the kids to see Santa Claus. You didn't need to dress so fancy," she said, shaking her head in wonder.

While it wasn't something she would wear, Gillian tried to be understanding that it was one of her mother's habits to dress like that. In the end, it was probable no one would notice so it really wasn't worth making a big deal out of.

"One should always look one's best, Gillian," her mother advised with her sheepish smile. "But if you think it's inappropriate I suppose I could change."

Gillian looked up in surprise; it wasn't like her mother to offer to change anything, especially her choice of clothing for the day.

"It's fine Mom, I'm sure no one will notice." Gillian said apologetically. She glanced down at her own jeans and comfy sweatshirt and tried to push away the feeling of being underdressed.

Before anything more was said, there was a deafening wave of children squealing with excitement, together with feet pounding on bare floorboards. Gillian hurried to the office door to greet the eager children.

"Now, now, children. Quiet, down!" she said with an excited laugh of her own. There was no denying that today was going to be a fun day.

Out of the corner of her eye Gillian could see her mother checking her makeup.

"Are they always this rowdy?" Maggie asked in a low voice.

"Of course not. They're just excited, that's all." Gillian

assured her Mom. "Now, if everyone is ready, let's get in line children. I'll be at the front and Aunt Maggie here will be at the back. Everyone must keep between us, is that understood?"

All the children replied in unison, "Yes, Aunt Gillian."

Gillian checked to make sure that her mother had taken her spot at the back of the line. While she didn't look entirely miserable, she sort of reminded Gillian of one of the children, unsure of what to do.

Gillian became lost in her thoughts as they loaded the kids in the van and started on their way to the mall. She enjoyed having her mother around, but the stress that she brought with her was palpable. Gillian couldn't remember a time, since she was a little girl, that she'd been able to just relax around her mom.

She had always scolded her about her behavior and how it would affect her father's campaign. She was right of course, as the Mayor's family, they were constantly gawked at and everything they did was nitpicked by the media.

Gillian remembered how she had thought it was neat to be the Mayor's daughter at one time. That had been when it had meant having more friends at school and a chauffeur to take her everywhere she wanted to go.

But when she had started realizing that neither of her parents really had time for her and even the wrong fashion choice had her on the front of the newspaper, she hadn't thought being the Mayor's daughter was so great anymore.

Now that she was an adult, Gillian realized her mother had taken on a lot of the stressful responsibility that even she hadn't felt the weight of, and because of this, she'd always tried to be patient with her mom, even when it was extra difficult.

Gillian stared out the window and tuned out the voices of the chattering children. She wondered what it would be like to have a family with Kevin. If they had children, would she be a better mother than her own?

She hoped so. If she couldn't be a better mother, than she

definitely didn't want to have children. It wasn't the children's fault after all what their parents decided to do with themselves and their lives. They were just along for the ride.

"We're here! We're here!" the children's excited squeals filled the van, bringing Gillian's mind back to the present.

Her thoughts about her hypothetical children would have to wait. She had an entire van full of children that were waiting to see Santa Clause and she was sure no one was going to be able to stop them from doing so.

---*---

Maggie gingerly stepped from the van. The ride had been rambunctious and loud and she hadn't even been close enough to Gillian to carry on a conversation. Not that the distance would have made a difference. It appeared Gillian had been deep in thought the entire ride over.

She had looked so sad, staring out the window in silence. It had made Maggie want to demand to know what was wrong. Of course, it seemed Gillian had stopped telling her what was wrong a long time ago.

"Can I hold your hand?" A small voice at her side surprised Maggie into a full stop.

"Why don't you hold hands with one of the other children?" Maggie answered somewhat uncertainly. She wasn't exactly sure what her role with the children was. She had only visited them a few times and not recently enough to see any of them twice. She wasn't sure she wanted them thinking this was a normal thing when it certainly wasn't.

The little boy who had asked, stared up at her with large brown eyes. They reminded Maggie of a puppy Gillian had begged to keep when she was little.

Black unruly hair fell over his face, contrasting nicely with his tanned skin. If she had to guess, Maggie would say he was seven or eight years old.

"I don't have a partner because there are only seven of us." Without waiting any longer, the little boy slipped his hand into Maggie's.

Maggie was surprised by the gesture but didn't want to fall any further behind so she started walking again to catch up with the rest of the group.

"I suppose you can for now," she said hesitantly.

As they walked, Maggie felt increasingly uncomfortable. The little boy on the other hand seemed overjoyed as he walked with a large smile on his face as if proud of his accomplishment at getting her to hold his hand.

Since the van was such a large vehicle it had to be parked at the back of the parking lot. It seemed that despite the fact that Gillian had made a reservation for the children to see Santa it hadn't kept other shoppers away. The lot was packed full of cars of every shape, color and size.

"What's your name?" Maggie finally asked her little companion. She had grown utterly weary of the stressed silence between them and the fact that it didn't seem to bother the little boy. It certainly bothered her.

"My name's Raymond, but everyone calls me Ray. What about yours?" the little boy asked happily flashing his white teeth in a smile and bouncing in place.

"Maggie," she answered hesitantly.

"Oh, I remember now! Aunt Gillian told us earlier." Ray nodded his head as if he were swallowing the information somewhere deep in his brain, never to be forgotten again.

After what seemed like forever and what Maggie was sure was fifty questions from Ray, they arrived at the little decorative booth set up for Santa inside the mall.

Maggie glanced down at Ray for the hundredth time. He was a smart little boy. She had to admire his constant desire to know the answers to his questions, no matter how annoying they were.

While Maggie would never admit it, in some ways, it was

kind of nice to have someone care about her opinion again, even if it was a little orphan boy who she would most likely never see again.

Gillian had all the children lined up behind her with Maggie and Raymond bringing up the rear. "Here we are, guys. We have to wait a few minutes for Santa to get himself settled and then you can all go in one by one and tell him what you'd like for Christmas," Gillian said with a big smile.

If Maggie didn't know better, she would think that Gillian was just as excited for the opportunity to see Santa as the fidgeting line of children.

Maggie felt an urgent tug on her hand and looked down to see Ray with a worried look on his little face.

"What now?" she asked, slightly worried about what he wanted to know this time. She had answered practically every question on the sun.

"Would you come in with me?" Raymond asked softly.

"Why? What do you need me for?" Maggie hadn't thought Ray would be the type to be afraid. After all, he hadn't been afraid of her and she had been a perfect stranger to him this morning.

"He might be scary," Ray said a little too loudly.

"It's just Santa. He's not scary," Maggie reassured him, patting his hand awkwardly with her free one.

Some of the other children had turned their heads to listen. Suddenly they weren't all fighting about who got to go first. Maggie wondered why they had the notion that he might be scary. Wasn't Santa portrayed to be a fun laughing man who brought presents to everyone?

"Look, there's no need to be afraid, he's just a man like all of us dressed up to look like Santa. There's not really a Santa, you know," Maggie said with a sigh. If that didn't put their minds at ease, she wasn't sure what would.

A collective gasp went up from all the children and Gillian who was now giving her a most disapproving glare.

Maggie suddenly realized that she'd been talking loudly

enough for everyone to hear instead of just Ray. Her cheeks blushed red as she realized her mistake.

"Mom!" Gillian half whispered from above the heads of the seven other children.

"Aunt Maggie has just never seen the real Santa. That's why she said that," Gillian's voice was strained as she tried to re-assure the children.

"But what if he's not real either?" A timid four year old said as she burst into tears.

Maggie watched as Gillian rushed to the little girl's side and tried to comfort her as several other children began to sniffle.

"Mom!" Gillian hissed now that she was close enough to Maggie to not be heard by all the kids. "How could you?"

"I- I thought-" Maggie stammered, unable to come up with the reasoning behind her slip up.

A strong tug on her hand pulled Maggie's attention away from the crying children and Gillian's effort to comfort them. Ray looked up at her with a disapproving look on his face.

"They don't know Santa's not real! You're not supposed to tell them," he scolded softly.

"Oh," Maggie said softly in disbelief. She had been completely unaware that such a simple comment could cause such uproar.

Just when Maggie thought that nothing could be fixed, out of the grotto came a rather tall man, all dressed in red. *Obviously the 'pretend' Santa Clause*, Maggie thought to herself.

"Now, now," he said in a loud but friendly voice. "What's all this? Children crying outside my grotto?"

"Sorry Santa," Gillian answered. "But somebody mentioned you might not be real."

Maggie noticed that Gillian had looked directly at her when she'd referred to somebody.

"Are you really Santa?" a little boy sniffled taking a step out of line.

"Of course I am," answered Santa, ruffling the little boy's hair.

Another boy, a little older than the first stepped out of line, doubt on his face, "Is that beard real? If I pull it will it come off?" he asked cautiously.

"Ho, ho, ho," said Santa laughing, his belly jiggling with the motion. "Of course, it's real. "Here," Santa pushed out his chin towards his second doubter. "Give it a good tug."

The young boy grabbed the beard and tugged. Much to Maggie's surprise it did not move; in fact, the pull brought tears to Santa's eyes.

"Satisfied?" asked Santa wiping away the tears with a large white handkerchief he'd taken from his pocket.

"Wow," said the older boy, his eyes as wide as saucers. "You really are Santa Claus."

"Come on, kids! Why don't you all come into my grotto and tell me what you want for Christmas."

He went into the grotto and the children looked expectantly at Gillian who gave them the signal to follow Santa. Once they were out of earshot, Gillian turned to Maggie.

"What were you thinking?" she said accusingly.

"You know I'm not good with kids," was all Maggie could think to say in her defense.

"I can tell," Gillian said with a sigh as one child came out of the grotto, and another hurried in.

"Gillian, I-"

Before Maggie could finish, Gillian hurried off towards a ruckus that had broken out near the entrance of the grotto.

Maggie felt movement at her side and looked down. She hadn't realized Ray was still holding her hand. His serious face stared back at her.

Somehow, Maggie felt that he knew something was wrong between her and Gillian.

They stood like that for some time before all the children had

had their turn and then it was Ray's. Apparently he had decided Santa wasn't so scary after all and let go of Maggie's hand to catch his turn.

As Maggie watched him go she was surprised to find she missed his sticky little hand in hers. She had messed today up but she wasn't sorry she had come. She hadn't realized how truly out of touch she was with everything and with other people and the only way she could start putting her life back together was by living it.

Chapter 5

Maggie paced uncomfortably outside the grotto, Ray must've had a long list because he was taking twice as long as all of the other children. Finally, Ray emerged, a huge smile on his tan little face.

After a few more words to the kids and more "ho ho ho's!" it was time to go.

"Thank you, Santa," Gillian said to the older gentleman. "It was really good of you to see the children."

"My pleasure my dear. Ho, ho ho," he laughed and again the belly jiggled.

"Come on, guys. Let's head back home." Gillian gathered the children in two's. Maggie silently took her place at the rear and much to her surprise, so did Ray, slipping his hand back into hers without even asking for permission this time.

Maggie couldn't help a little smile coming to her lips. At least one person wasn't upset about her earlier slip up.

They all filed back to the van, the children merrily chatting to each other about Santa Claus and what presents they'd asked for.

Gillian and Maggie both stayed silent, but just as on the ride there, Maggie was pretty sure they wouldn't have been able to talk much on the ride anyway.

Ray sat next to Maggie and he too was silent, his intelligent eyes filled with thought as he took turns staring out the window and staring at Maggie, making her uncomfortable. Maggie breathed a sigh of relief as they finally reached the orphanage and the children filed out to go tell anyone who would listen about their experience.

"See ya next time!" Ray called over his shoulder as he raced up the steps of the orphanage. Maggie offered a little wave in return. She didn't have the heart right now to tell him there might not be a next time.

"You're still upset," Maggie said softly putting a hand on Gillian's arm to stop her from going into the house.

27

Gillian pulled away. "I'm not upset Mom. I just thought today would go different, that's all," Gillian sighed and glanced up at the orphanage.

"You know, you haven't really been there for a lot of things I care about and the kids are important to me. I just thought now that you have more time, you'd take more of an interest." Gillian looked down at her hands and a red blush filled her cheeks.

"I am interested Gillian. That's why I'm here. And I've always tried to be there for you," Maggie added quickly. She had never been one of those mothers who neglected their children, had she?

"Growing up you were always so busy with Dad and his next big project. Do you even remember taking me to see Santa?" Gillian glanced up at her and Maggie was surprised to see the hurt in her blue eyes.

"I-" Maggie paused. The truth was, she didn't remember taking Gillian to see Santa a single time. "I never meant to leave you out," Maggie finally said, defeated.

"I know Mom, but I always went with my best friend from next door when her mom took her to see Santa, and I remember the one thing I always asked him for was for you to take me the next year, but you never did."

Tears formed in Gillian's eyes and Maggie couldn't bear to watch any longer.

"I'm sorry Gillian, I never knew-" Maggie reached out and placed an awkward hand on her daughter's shoulder.

They stood like that for several moments until Gillian had wiped her tears away.

"I'm just glad we are seeing each other now. Let's not waste our time, okay? Do you want to stay for lunch?" Gillian forced a brave smile that made Maggie feel even worse. She suddenly felt as if every illusion of being a good parent had fallen away and left only the bare ugly reality.

"Sure, I'll stay," she finally said in a defeated voice.

Gillian nodded and headed toward the house. This time Maggie didn't try to stop her. She had so much to think about, it was going to take a while before she was ready to have another deep conversation with her daughter.

When Maggie finally made her way into the orphanage she was surprised to see Ray sitting in one of the large armchairs in the living room.

She took a seat cautiously nearby.

"Are you staying for lunch?" he asked a little timidly.

"Yes, Gillian invited me," Maggie said shifting a little. She wondered if Ray had heard their conversation through the big window that was wide open, letting sunlight stream in over them both.

"Why don't you believe in Santa?" Maggie asked, surprising herself.

"Well, I always ask for the same thing every year, always, and I do try to be really good, but I never get what I ask for," Ray said with a sad look on his face that filled Maggie with sympathy.

"What do you ask for?" Maggie asked, a little unsure about the direction of the conversation.

"Well, I always ask Santa to give me a family, but I guess either I'm not good enough, or Santa's not real, or both," Ray looked away.

For a child so young, Maggie hadn't expected him to have such dreary thoughts.

"Why ever would you think you're not good enough?" Maggie truly wanted to know. Of all things, Ray certainly shouldn't be thinking he wasn't good enough for a family.

"Maybe my mom left because she thought I wasn't good enough," Ray said somberly.

"You mustn't think like that, Ray. Adults are complicated and sometimes have complicated problems, but whatever reason your mom had that caused her to leave wasn't because you weren't good

29

enough," Maggie said strongly.

"Then why did my mom leave?" Ray looked at Maggie with a face begging for answers that Maggie wasn't sure she could give.

She suddenly felt unsure of herself and didn't want to continue this conversation but she felt as if she had no choice.

"Maybe your mom was sick. Sometimes when moms get sick or other things happen, they can't care very well for their children so they try to send them to a family that can do a better job than they can."

Maggie hoped that her explanation made Ray feel a little better.

"Then why don't I have a family?" Ray asked.

Maggie sighed. Somehow, she didn't have a good answer for that one. The fact that no one had adopted Ray yet broke her heart.

"I don't know Ray, but I do know that one day you will have a wonderful family that will take care of you and love you until you are older than me," Maggie said with a little chuckle.

Ray's little eyes lit up a bit and he sat a little straighter.

"Do you really think so?"

"I know so," Maggie said as the lunch bell rang throughout the orphanage. As she watched Ray skipping down the hall, she hoped she hadn't been wrong. If anyone deserved a family, Ray did.

Chapter 6

When Maggie walked into the dining room she was surprised to see a tall older gentleman kneeling down talking to Ray. While she didn't frequent the orphanage by any stretch of the imagination, she still knew everyone who worked there and had never seen this man before.

Whoever he was, Ray seemed to be quite familiar with him but then again, Ray seemed to be quite outgoing.

Upon seeing Maggie, the man stood up and made his way over to her to within a few steps.

"It's nice to meet you after hearing so much about you," he said with a deep voice.

"It's nice to meet you too-" Maggie paused as they shook hands. She wasn't sure what this man's name was or without sounding rude, how to ask. She had caused enough ruckus for one day and didn't wish to incite any more.

"Geoffrey Lawson," the man said, shaking her hand with a firm confident energy that startled her. Maggie noticed he was quite an attractive man, not too young; most likely in his fifty's or early sixties. Still, he looked well preserved.

For some reason he looked oddly familiar in some way but Maggie couldn't quite place it.

"Mr. Lawson, will you sit by me for lunch?" Ray asked tugging on Mr. Lawson's sleeve.

"Sure thing, little man," Mr. Lawson said with a laugh. Soon they were all seated around the large dining room table with foam plates piled high with hot dogs and chips sitting in front of them.

It wasn't a meal that Maggie would eat normally but she decided not to complain as she caught a stern glance from both Gillian and Ray.

"You know, you look like that Santa Claus we saw today," Ray said around a large bite of hotdog. "Except without a beard," he said it in a very matter of fact way as if he had thought he might be questioned further if he wasn't confident in his answer.

"I am no Santa Claus," Mr. Lawson said with a chuckle as he winked at Maggie above Raymond's head.

For a moment, Maggie wasn't sure she had understood but then it dawned on her. No wonder Mr. Lawson seemed so familiar. He was the fake Santa from the mall.

Maggie couldn't help but give a small knowing smile, he had fooled them all well, how, she had no idea, but he had certainly seemed real enough. He had almost convinced her and that was saying something.

Despite her earlier doubts, the hotdogs and chips were delicious and Maggie even had a second one which earned her a proud nod from Ray.

When lunch was over she felt almost sad that the day was drawing to a close and she would be heading back to her lonely apartment.

After the children had all left to wash up and move on with their day, Maggie and Mr. Lawson remained in the dining room alone. A sudden silence settled over the quite room, making Maggie nervous once more.

"Was there something Mr. Lawson wanted?"

"Looks like Ray has taken quite a liking to you. He's quite the special little boy," Mr. Lawson said at last, rubbing his hands up and down on his jeans pockets.

"I suppose he is," Maggie said uncertainly. She wasn't sure why Mr. Lawson had stuck around to talk after lunch. It wasn't as if she knew him or anything.

"So that was you at the mall," she observed. Now as Maggie looked closely, she could almost visualize Mr. Lawson with his fake beard and fake round jiggly belly.

"How did you manage the trick with the beard? It looked so realistic."

Mr. Lawson gave a laugh that reminded Maggie even more of

the fake Santa. "Oh, well, I couldn't find the special glue that came with the costume, so I used some I had in a drawer. Turned out to be stronger than I thought."

"How did you get it off?" Maggie couldn't contain her curiosity.

"I had to soak my chin in white spirit," Geoffrey confessed with a small chuckle and an embarrassed look.

"Well, no wonder it's so red," Maggie said with a little laugh.

"It's not that funny," Mr. Lawson reprimanded.

"What about the stomach?" Maggie asked skeptically. It was so odd how he had looked to have a round jiggly belly and now he was as skinny as she was herself.

"Oh, a man can't give away all his secrets," Mr. Lawson chuckled.

Maggie searched around the room for her purse.

"Looking for this?" he held up the missing handbag with a charming smile.

"Thank you, Mr. Lawson," Maggie said gratefully.

"No need for formalities! Just call me Geoffrey." he said with a laugh.

"I noticed you wore Ralph Lauren to a children's trip. Not a lot of people would choose that outfit," Geoffrey said with a puzzled look.

"How on earth do you know this is a Ralph Lauren?" Maggie was more intrigued by this than she was annoyed by the comment.

"My ex-wife bought enough Ralph Lauren to bankrupt me. I'd know his clothes anywhere."

Maggie was even more confused by Geoffrey than ever and the fact that she had never heard him mentioned before. "Oh," was all she could think to say.

"Do you come to the orphanage often?" Geoffrey asked after a few more moments of silence between them.

"Not really, and usually I just come to see my daughter." Maggie fidgeted under his intense stare.

"Well that would explain the whole not believing in Santa incident." Geoffrey nodded his head in a thoughtful manner.

"You know, I didn't know the children were such adamant believers and I never meant to upset everyone," Maggie said honestly.

She didn't know what it was about Geoffrey that made her feel she could talk to him.

"The only reason I came today was to spend time with my daughter but it seems that I messed things up a little more with her as well," Maggie sighed.

"I'm sure Gillian will get over it if she's even still upset. She's a wonderful young woman and if anyone might understand, it would be her."

Maggie only nodded at Geoffrey's kind words. Hopefully he was right.

"I should probably get going," she said reluctantly. For some reason she suddenly wanted to stay, but as usual she couldn't find the words to say so.

Geoffrey opened the dining room door for her in such a way that she had to walk under his arm to get out. He was so tall, she didn't even have to duck. As she passed under his arm he mumbled something to her.

"Sorry, did you say something?" Maggie turned to ask him.

"I, erm, I just wondered if you might be free for dinner one evening." He stammered.

"Why?" she asked voicing the question in her mind before she could think about it.

Geoffrey took his hand off the door and it sprung closed behind him. They were both now standing in the large hallway.

"I just thought that as we are both single, and you are quite interesting to have a conversation with, we might enjoy spending an evening together." Geoffrey said with a shrug.

"How did you know I'm *single*?" She was suddenly not sure how she felt about the title. It hadn't been that long since her marriage with Leonard had fallen apart and to be honest with herself, a new relationship wasn't something she was sure she was ready for.

"Oh. I'm sorry," he said, "I didn't realize, Gillian said you were divorced so I just assumed."

"It's fine. I mean I am, I'm just not sure I'm ready for a new relationship at the moment after…" Maggie stopped unable to finish her sentence.

"I didn't mean to pressure you, but if you change your mind, here's my card."

Maggie accepted the small white card that Geoffrey offered her. She placed it neatly inside her purse and with a final nod, headed out to where the taxi was already waiting. She wasn't sure she was ready for dinner with Geoffrey any time soon, but one never knew. Maybe one of these days she would find herself in need of company and call him.

On the ride home, she thought about everything that had happened. It was a lot to take in. Spending time with Gillian had been fun in a way but she had also learned some things about her daughter and about herself that she wasn't sure she was too happy about.

It was going to take a lot more work to repair their relationship than she had thought.

But Maggie was determined. After all, that was one relationship in her life she still had a chance of saving.

Chapter 7

Gillian woke up with a start. She was sure she had heard something downstairs. Maybe one of the children had gotten up extra early and was getting into the Christmas ornaments downstairs. She had been meaning to get them hung up but they still were four weeks away from Christmas so she figured they still had time. She had been slowly gathering different decorations and putting them up around the house.

She knew that taking the kids to do their Santa visit so early on was a little rushed but she had explained that it would give Santa longer to find their gifts.

In a way it was true. She had searched for at least one item from each child's list that Geoffrey had provided her with once they had finished telling him.

Gillian made her way quietly down the stairs. It was still dark outside and even though she hadn't checked the clock she was pretty sure it was around four or five in the morning.

Finally she reached the living area and flicked on the lamp light. In its soft glow, she was able to make out a lone figure sitting on the sofa.

She knew who it was immediately by the telltale worn-out grey blanket that accompanied it, Ray.

"Ray, honey, what are you doing up this early in the morning?" She asked cautiously, taking a seat near the little boy.

"I couldn't sleep." Gillian could tell from the sniffle in his voice that he had been crying.

"Why couldn't you sleep?" she prodded gently, reaching down and pulling his little body up against hers in a hug.

"I had a nightmare," he said with a hitch in his voice. Ray looked up at her, his eyes full of glistening tears.

Gillian's heart went out to Ray. He had been abandoned on the orphanage doorstep when he was but a year old. The little toddler hadn't had so much as a note with him, leaving them to raise him. Gillian had always thought they would find him a family. He had been the most adorable toddler, but for some reason, every family who had considered him had passed him up for someone else.

"Aunt Gillian? Will my mom ever come back for me?" Ray's voice quivered as he asked the question he had asked since he began to talk.

"Ray, I think one day you will have a mother, but it may not be the same mother who brought you here. Do you understand?"

The one part of caring for the children in the orphanage that Gillian could hardly bear was explaining to them how they had ended up here. Some of them were old enough to remember, and one could always hope that they would find a family before they could begin to question where they came from, but it didn't always work out that way.

"I- I think so," Ray said with a sniffle.

"Let's get you back to bed," Gillian said affectionately, scooping him up into her arms.

He hugged her tight as she carried him back to the boy's room and deposited him gently into his bunk.

"Go to sleep Ray. I'll wait until you're sleeping to leave," Gillian whispered, being extra careful not to wake any of the other children.

Soon, Ray's breathing steadied out into long deep breaths and Gillian knew he was asleep.

Feeling sleepy herself, she hurried back toward her abandoned bed. As she rounded a corner in the hall she nearly ran Lorna over.

"Lorna! What are you doing up? You nearly gave me a heart attack!" she shrieked.

Lorna shushed her through a fit of giggles. While Gillian's heart was still beating wildly from the scare, she joined in with a soft giggle. The moment reminded her of something that schoolgirls would do as they snuck around their dorms undetected by teachers.

"The real question is what are you doing up. You're not usually such an early riser," Lorna said with a smile. It was true. There were some days that Gillian was the last one up in the house, but it was for good reason. She was also usually the last one asleep.

"Ray was down here in the living room. He had another nightmare, poor kiddo." Gillian shook her head in pity as she recounted to Lorna her little run in with Ray.

"If I were looking to keep one of the kids permanently, it would be Ray. He is such a sweetheart," Lorna agreed as Gillian finished.

Gillian wished that someone who was looking to adopt a child would think that way.

"You going back to sleep?" Lorna finally asked with an accusing look.

"Oh come on, don't judge! I need my beauty sleep to function," Gillian said, ignoring Lorna's eye roll as she resumed her path toward her bed once more.

She hoped she could get a few more hours of rest before everyone in the house woke up. Sighing, she snuggled down into her covers.

If she could really ask Santa for something, she would ask for a family for Ray. A little boy like him shouldn't suffer for lack of a family.

Gillian drifted off to sleep, thoughts of the many awaiting Christmas preparations on her mind.

Chapter 8

Maggie's thoughts kept returning to Ray from the orphanage as she cooked her lonely breakfast for one. It had been two days since she'd been to the orphanage and for some reason she had thought more than once of popping in and saying hello.

Maybe it was what her daughter said about their past, or maybe it was the little boy who didn't seem to care that she was an adult having serious issues in life, but for some reason she couldn't shake the place from her mind.

Maggie smiled softly. Perhaps this was the way Gillian had felt that had made her stay on at the orphanage full time.

She wasn't sure why Gillian had asked her to look after the children in the first place. She knew Maggie wasn't exactly a kid person. But maybe the children had done her good. It seemed that after so much time feeling sorry for herself or thinking of what she could have done differently, she had forgotten what it was like to think of others.

Maggie's thoughts went back to Ray again. He was a cute little boy that was for sure. Poor thing, thinking he was to blame for his mother's abandonment. How any parent could leave their children behind was beyond all reason to Maggie. While she had struggled to adjust with Gillian, she had become everything to her, no matter what Gillian said about her being too involved in her father's work. Gillian's needs always came first as far as Maggie was concerned.

Or at least that was the way Maggie had thought it had been. Maybe she was thinking of the wrong needs. Maybe she had focused too much on what she thought Gillian needed rather than looking closely at what she really needed. Maggie chuckled to herself as she remembered the time she was supposed to host a small dinner party for some important people who Leonard was hoping to convince to financially support his campaign. It was around Christmas and she had taken Gillian shopping for a new dress to wear to the annual party they hosted for Leonard's staff members' children. When Maggie couldn't find anything to her liking in her usual stores, she decided at the last minute to take her to a new designer in Manhattan that she had heard of. Maggie had become so enthralled by all the beautiful designs, she completely lost track of time. Thank goodness Leonard's ever faithful assistant had come to his rescue and had taken care of the food without the guests even knowing of her absence. Maggie remembered Leonard's face when she'd come rushing in the front door with a sleeping Gillian in her arms. He hadn't let her forget that little faux pas for a long time.

Maggie's smile turned into a frown as the thought of Leonard surfaced. She thought of him often, more often than she'd like to. She wondered if he was happy with the young woman they had broken up over. She wondered if they were still together.

There were days when Maggie wondered what it would be like to call Leonard and reconcile things between them, but pride stood in her way. It had been almost seven weeks now and he hadn't called her. If he had wanted her to stay, shouldn't he have tried a little harder to keep her?

Maggie wondered if there ever would be another man in her life. She really wasn't sure she could see that happening. She wasn't sure what she would do if she got in a relationship where she was the complete opposite. What if they didn't have anything in common but had already developed feelings for one another? If there was one thing she missed about Leonard, it was everything they had in common; watching adventure movies on the couch with extra buttered popcorn and peanut butter cookies, their dislike of cats and love of dogs, even though they hadn't had one in years, and the list went on.

No matter what Leonard had done, she kept remembering the Leonard she fell in love with, not the man who had cheated on her. He had in the end come out and told her about it, he had said he wanted to stop, but she couldn't believe him. After so much time of being lied to, she couldn't trust anything he said.

She had felt like such a fool! She still did. She had gone on with her life, content that she had a faithful husband who loved her, and then found out that the affair had been going on for over five months at the office.

It wasn't unheard of. Maggie had lots of friends who had had it happen to them, but she had never imagined it could happen to her.

So far, this had become a really bad day and she hadn't even eaten breakfast yet. Maggie sighed and served up the scrambled eggs and bacon with two pieces of apple onto a simple glass plate. She placed two pieces of whole wheat toast beside it.

As she ate, she stared at the phone. She was nearly half through her breakfast before she convinced herself to call Gillian.

"Mom?" the surprise in Gillian's voice nearly made Maggie hang up. Since when had it become something so surprising for her to call her daughter? The truth was, she couldn't remember the last time she had called just because. Well there was that one time for Christmas, but that had been to wish her a Merry Christmas.

"Hi Gillian, I was just calling to say hello," Maggie said, nearly choking on a bite of egg. Maybe she should have waited until she had finished eating.

"Okay, well hi Mom," Gillian said with a little chuckle.

"Come on Gillian, I know I don't call often, but I'd like to change that, after all, that's what I bought a cellphone for, right?"

"No, you're right Mom. I was just surprised, that's all." Another pause followed Gillian's confession.

"Do you want to come over this evening? We're having movie night with the kids," Gillian asked tentatively.

For a moment, Maggie felt tempted to turn her down. After all, she didn't want Gillian to feel like she had to invite her just because she had called. But one look around the lonely empty apartment convinced her otherwise.

"Sure, I guess I'm not doing anything tonight," Maggie said trying not to sound too excited.

When had she become so desperate to spend time with other human beings?

Maybe living in an apartment all alone for six weeks thinking about the mistakes of your past did that to you.

"Great! We'll see you tonight then, and thanks for calling." Gillian sounded truly happy and this in turn made Maggie make a mental note to call her daughter more often.

If she had been absent in her daughter's life, it couldn't be too soon to try to start fixing it.

"Okay, see you tonight then. Bye," Maggie said uncertainly.

Now that she was aware of the rift between her and her daughter, their interactions seemed awkward. Maggie couldn't help feeling that she was doing something wrong but was unable to fix it due to not knowing exactly what it was.

"Bye Mom," Gillian said softly, and the click of the phone followed.

Maggie stared at the silent phone with a smile. Maybe she was making progress, or maybe she was just starting to realize things around her that she had been too busy to see before.

She finished her breakfast, tidying up in record time then sat down at her sofa and stared around the living room.

Now that her boxes weren't threatening her with needing unpacking, she felt an overwhelming sense of boredom and uncertainty of what to do. Her eyes landed on her running shoes. It had also been nearly two days since she'd gone running; she just hadn't felt the inspiration to do so.

The idea didn't seem too bad at the time, despite having just eaten. Maybe she could just go for a light jog to pass the time. After all, she hadn't really had time to explore the nearby park much.

Maggie slipped her shoes on and flexed her feet. They felt right, like something in her life that had remained constant despite all of the other changes.

After changing into some appropriate running clothes, she headed out the door with a big smile on her face. She had a feeling that it had to do with recent developments with her social life, but for some reason she felt happy and right no matter what the past haunted her with. She listened to the pitter patter of her shoes on the sidewalk as she ran towards the park. Everything was going to be okay now. She was sure of it.

Chapter 9

The rhythm of running relaxed Maggie in a way that no other activity could. She had been a runner since she was a teenager on the track team, and it was still her favorite thing to do. It seemed odd to many people that a woman as old as herself enjoyed running so much. Maggie actually enjoyed their shocked looks when they saw her jogging through the neighborhood or making her way toward the finish line at a marathon in town.

"Fancy seeing you here!" A low voice made her running rhythm skip a beat.

She swiveled her head trying to find the owner of the voice that seemed to be addressing her. As she turned in the other direction and spotted the speaker, a wave of unknown emotion washed over her. She found herself face to face with Geoffrey who was running at an even pace, not two strides behind her. He wore a gray hoodie and sweat pants, complimented by running shoes not unlike her own.

"Geoffrey?" she exclaimed, not quite able to believe her eyes. She had noticed that he had seemed fit but she wouldn't have guessed he took up running and the odds he would be out at the same time as her were quite unusual.

"The one and only!" Geoffrey said with a chuckle. "Don't look so shocked. You know, I'm surprised we haven't run into each other before. I come here every single day and have never seen you out here." Geoffrey was able to make his statement without missing a step or a breath.

"I- I've only been to this park a handful of times," Maggie defended herself.

"We seem to be going about the same pace and in the same direction. Do you mind if I tag along?" Geoffrey asked politely.

It took Maggie a moment, but she finally answered with a little smile, "That would be fine."

While she hadn't decided about having a relationship per say with Geoffrey, he was right about their direction and speed, and it had been a long time since Maggie had had someone to run with. She enjoyed having that natural built in competition when you were running beside someone and occasionally a good conversation would come along with that competition.

"I didn't know you liked to run," Maggie said after they had continued on for several moments in silence.

"Well, I didn't always love it, but then I needed something to keep my waist down and learned to love it over time." Geoffrey glanced over at her with a mischievous smile. "What about you? Are you a natural runner or do you do it because you need to?" Geoffrey seemed to realize that his wording was off at the same time that Maggie did, and they burst out laughing together causing several other joggers to glance their way.

"I'm a natural runner, always loved it, most likely always will," Maggie said as they continued down the path.

"I'm glad we ran into each other, running is much nicer when you have someone to share it with," Geoffrey said in that low voice of his.

Maggie almost agreed out loud but decided she would keep her thoughts to herself. She didn't want Geoffrey getting any wrong ideas about her.

---*---

"Did you like the movie Aunt Maggie? Ray's little hand was tugging on her sleeve only moments after the credits started rolling.

"I did. It was quite entertaining," Maggie responded smiling down at Ray. She was surprised to find that it was a genuine smile and response. She had enjoyed the movie more than she had enjoyed anything in a while. She smoothed back Ray's black hair, it was something that she had always done with Gillian when she was a girl and having Ray so close to her had awoken something from her past.

"I'm gonna get us more popcorn," Ray said happily before running off in the direction of the snack table.

"Ray's taken quite a liking to you, Mom," Gillian said with a chuckle.

Maggie took a sip of her punch, "I suppose so. He's one special little kid. Any possibility of a family for him soon?" she asked hopefully.

Gillian shook her head sadly, "I'm afraid not. There have been lots of people looking for kids. I guess they have all just taken different ones than Ray."

"Speaking of absent parents, have you talked to your father?" Maggie wasn't sure why she asked the question. Maybe it was because when you spent twenty-five years with someone it was hard to just forget about them completely without looking back.

"I actually haven't. I saw him about a week after the divorce, but since then he hasn't been answering my calls and no one has really seen him much." Gillian sighed, and Maggie could sense that she was sad about her father's lack of communication.

"You know how he gets caught up in his work. Most likely he misplaced his phone. Your father was always losing things." Maggie gave a little chuckle as she thought of it.

Leonard had always been looking for something, whether it had been his phone or his wallet. She had always scheduled ten minutes extra when they were going to go somewhere to give him time to search for said item. She couldn't count all the times they had arrived a little late or been rushing to get to a place because of an extended search.

"I am glad you came today, and the kids enjoyed having you too, especially Ray." Gillian changed the subject flawlessly. Maggie smiled, Gillian had always been a good peacekeeper and good at distracting you if that was what you needed.

"I'm glad I came too. I think it did me good," Maggie said, watching Ray try to stuff a few too many popcorn kernels into his already overflowing bowl.

"I think I'll go help him with that," Maggie said, once again speaking before she could think.

"Have fun Mom, and you know you can come by anytime. We are always more than happy to have you," Gillian called after her as Maggie headed toward the snack table.

Maggie smiled to herself, maybe she would take Gillian up on that offer. She actually found herself liking the orphanage more and more as she spent time there. Maybe it was the kids, the company or maybe it was just that time of year.

Chapter 10

Geoffrey struggled with his cufflinks as he prepared himself for a night out. He didn't have a date or anything, but he enjoyed going out and enjoying a decent meal at a restaurant occasionally, even if it was a meal alone.

Ever since his wife left, he had learned to fend for himself. His eyes traveled to the calendar on the wall. It had been nearly a year now.

"Going to find herself. I've never heard a worse excuse," he said to no one in particular as he shook his head.

He had asked her to stay, promising things would be different, but of course as stubborn as she had been, she'd refused to listen or even consider his pleas. Geoffrey shook his head, it wasn't that he had exactly looked for a new relationship in the last year, but he hadn't really been waiting around for Anna's return either.

He often wondered if she was finding what she had wanted to find so badly. When she occasionally sent an email, it was typically a couple of lines of text and just a bare description of what city or beach she was visiting. He wondered if one day she would come back and want to be back in his life. He wasn't sure, and more than that he wasn't sure if he was ready to let her back into his life. He knew that their marriage had been falling apart, but that didn't mean he didn't or hadn't loved her. Things were just complicated.

His thoughts settled on Maggie for a moment. It had been a while since he had meet someone like her. While she was easily in her fifties, there was a bounce to her that let everyone know she wasn't quite done with her life yet. He liked that about her; the energy she portrayed. Nothing could get her down.

She seemed reluctant to go out with him though. This was something new for Geoffrey but under the circumstances, completely understandable. From what he'd heard it had been less than two months since Maggie had divorced her husband.

Whether Maggie Faulkner was willing to give him a chance in a relationship or not, he was definitely willing to pursue a friendship. He hadn't had so much fun on his afternoon jogs as he had the other day in longer than he could remember.

He gave a little chuckle as he thought back to some of the jokes they'd shared. There seemed to be a natural chemistry between them, whether Maggie was ready to explore it or not. With his cufflinks finally in place and his suitcoat ready to go, Geoffrey headed out the door. His stomach was growling and he couldn't wait to visit his favorite Italian restaurant. Maybe he would even hit the theater afterward, who knew?

Taking one last look around his apartment he closed the door with a final click and turned the key in the lock. He wasn't going to be that man who waited in his apartment for years, waiting for the person they used to love. He was going to go on living his life and take problems as they came, one at a time.

Maggie closed and reopened her fridge. She wasn't even sure what all she had in the fridge. Why she had bought such a large fancy fridge, she had no idea. Maybe it was just the urge to make her apartment feel a little fuller. The fridge had every type of leftover inside of it. Whenever Maggie wanted to eat something, she had come to depend on there being some lost little morsel inside her fridge. She also knew that she needed to clean it out. She was sure that there was some new species of mold manifesting itself on the leftovers from the pizza she had bought her first night in the apartment.

Despite usually being able to find something to snack on, tonight, she was unsuccessful. There was nothing that looked appetizing or edible and certainly nothing that met both of those criteria.

Maybe she should take herself out to a nice restaurant and spoil herself with a lovely meal. Of course, it wasn't something she had done before. She wasn't sure that it was something she wanted to try on her own. It might be the usual thing to do these days for some women, but Maggie was still a little old fashioned at heart. She didn't mind going to a coffee house on her own, or even for a spot of light lunch but she had always considered going out to a restaurant for a fancy dinner an activity for two.

For a moment, Geoffrey's card in her purse tempted her. She had certainly enjoyed their jog together the other day. She shook her head in a silent answer to her question. She wasn't that desperate.

She could call Gillian sometime and they could go out together, but that wouldn't fix her dilemma for tonight. Gillian had told her on movie night that she wouldn't be around the next two evenings; something about staff meetings and manager responsibilities. Besides that, Maggie didn't want to wear out her new welcome with her daughter. She knew that it had taken several years for their relationship to deteriorate and that she may need to be willing to give it at least that much time to recuperate.

Right now, though, she was starving, and she really wasn't keen on eating yet another meal alone with the fake people on the television. Maggie scolded herself once more as she thought of the television. It hadn't been a necessary purchase and she wasn't sure what had possessed her when she'd bought it. "Something to keep you company," the store salesman had said. For some reason Maggie had believed him and brought the slim Samsung flat screen home. It did give her apartment a certain modern look that she wasn't that opposed to, but as far as company? That part had been a lie. Maggie didn't feel any less lonely with the TV on than she did without it.

Everyone always seemed to be turning to their electronic devices these days. What was wrong with a good book? What happened to the days when teenagers would rush home to see what chapter they could get to before it was time for bed? She wasn't sure where those days had gone for the rest of the world, but for her, she still couldn't resist a good read.

Maggie paused and listened for any type of sound, but besides a lone motor passing on the streets outside, nothing greeted her awaiting ears.

"That's enough, I've got to get out and do something myself before I drive myself crazy," she said forcefully to the quietness.

She hurried to her room and changed into something appropriate for a date. While she didn't have a partner, she was still going to look presentable. That was half of the restaurant experience. As she headed out the door, she thought about how it was funny that she'd stopped doing something she'd done in the past at least three times a week. Maggie hadn't been to a restaurant since her divorce. Before then, even up until the last couple of crazy months of their marriage, she and Leonard had gone to dinner together frequently. They had made it a point to try out nearly every reputable place in their town and nearly succeeded too. Some nights they would settle for something they knew was good to avoid the possibility of disappointment should they pick a bad place.

She wondered if he took his new woman out to their special restaurants. She hated to think of Leonard sitting in their special booth together with another woman enjoying a meal. She blinked her eyes quickly, hating that they'd begun to fill with tears. It was too soon for her to be able to think of such things without getting emotional. People said it would get better with time, but it had been nearly eight months now; six months separated while they were married and two months divorced, and it still didn't feel any better.

As Maggie stepped outside of the apartment building, she looked up and down the sidewalk. She was sure she had seen a little Italian place just down the street from there somewhere; she just wasn't sure in which direction. She remembered seeing it the day she came to look over the apartment with the agent. In fact, it was one of things the agent mentioned to her as a reason to rent the apartment. Funny, but she'd never thought about it again till now.

After a few moments of arguing with herself, she chose to go to the right. She remembered it was only a short walk to the restaurant and figured that it wouldn't take too long to backtrack if it was indeed to the left. After walking only a few blocks she saw the small Italian sign lighting up the street. She breathed a sigh of relief. She had chosen the right direction.

As she approached, she began to think maybe she should have called first to see if they had a table. The thought of turning back crossed her mind. Not only would it be embarrassing to ask for a table of one, but for them not to have room for another person in the restaurant and to be turned down in front of all those people? That would indeed be humiliating.

Maggie knew she was just making excuses to herself not to go in on her own, but she also knew that she had to do it one day. She couldn't spend the rest of her life not going to restaurants just because she didn't have a partner, or because they might be full, or because of whatever other excuse she had invented that evening. She stopped at the door and peeked in through the window. It looked nice enough and she breathed a sigh of relief as she spotted some empty tables towards the back. At least tonight she wouldn't be sent home hungry and alone. Suddenly the door sprung open and a rather portly gentleman with a large handlebar mustache and wide grin stood there.

"My dear lady," he spoke in a rather affected Italian accent. "Please come into my humble little restaurant."

Maggie struggled with the urge to giggle at what she was quite sure wasn't a real accent.

"Oh, erm, thank you," she stammered as she slowly entered passing him in the doorway. "That's very kind of you."

"Here you are my beautiful lady, the best a seat in the house." He pulled back a chair for her at a small table under a dimmed wall light. The table was already set for one. It had a red and white gingham tablecloth, as did all the tables, and these matched the little curtains at the window.

Maggie thanked the man and as she sat down, he handed her a menu before walking away. She studied the menu and had to admit it all looked very appetizing; certainly, more appetizing than anything she would have had in the refrigerator, had she stayed in.

"I see you like Italian too." The deep voice interrupted Maggie's reading. Even though she'd only heard it a few times she recognized it instantly. She looked up to see none other than Geoffrey. Her mouth seemed to take on a life of its own as she looked up at him and smiled. *Why did I do that?* She thought to herself still not able to remove the stupid smile.

"I'd ask if you came here often but I actually do and would have remembered if I'd seen you here before," Geoffrey said returning her smile.

"Well," Maggie answered regaining her composure. "You're right. I haven't been here before," she replied. She turned her attention back to looking at the menu.

"Would you mind if I join you?" asked Geoffrey. "It looks to me like you're just about to order."

"You're not here with anyone?" Maggie asked, surprised. For some reason she had thought that she was the only one in the predicament of going to a fancy dinner alone. Part of her hoped that he would insist on joining her and the other part hoped he would walk away and continue on with his own dinner.

"No, I am here alone, like you as I see. Maybe a bit of company would be nice. What do you say?" Geoffrey asked pleasantly.

Maggie lowered the menu and looked up at him.

"I-" Maggie paused suddenly, uncertain as to what she really wanted to happen next. Yes a little company would be nice, but this would be the second time she was spending time with Geoffrey in less than a week. The suddenness of it made her nervous.

"Roberto," Geoffrey called across to the waiter, "Would you bring another set of cutlery, please? I'm going to join my friend here."

The waiter moved to comply with Geoffrey's request before Maggie could say another word.

Maggie placed the menu down on the table and looked at

Geoffrey with a puzzled expression.

"Are you sure you didn't follow me here?" she asked.

"Of course, I didn't follow you here. What would make you think such an absurd thing?" Geoffrey asked as he sat down opposite her.

"It's just a little odd that we would happen to be in the same place at the same time twice in the same week," Maggie noted, truly puzzled.

"Either we have the same tastes and the same intuition on when to go out, or the universe just knows we need each other's company," Geoffrey said with a chuckle as he began to read the menu the waiter had brought him.

Geoffrey looked across at her as the waiter set the table in front of him and poured him a glass of water.

"Have you found anything that looks tasty?" asked Geoffrey, glancing down at his own menu.

Maggie shook her head as she looked back down at the menu.

"The lobster is really good here," Geoffrey said flipping a page.

"Really?" Maggie answered not taking her eyes off the menu, "I'm not really a lobster person. My family has always been slightly allergic." Maggie was surprised she had shared that information with Geoffrey. She wasn't one to talk about her family with people she didn't know well.

"They have a nice choice of wines also," Geoffrey said flipping yet another page.

"And the elephant roulade is to die for," Geoffrey pushed on.

This got Maggie's full attention. "Elephant?" she asked trying to stifle a smile.

"Just making sure you were listening," Geoffrey put his menu down. "Really anything they have here is delicious. It just depends on what you're in the mood for."

"Well so far, I haven't really found anything that just speaks to me on the menu," Maggie said with a sigh.

They both turned back to studying the menu and soon the waiter came over to take their order.

"Do you know what you would like, or should I give you another minute?" he asked and Maggie couldn't help but notice he didn't make such a big deal about the Italian accent this time.

Neither her nor Geoffrey said anything for several moments and then in unison they said, "Fettuccini Alfredo,"

Maggie looked over at Geoffrey and they burst out laughing. Geoffrey turned to the waiter.

"I think that will be two Fettuccini Alfredo, please Roberto."

Maggie watched the waiter go with a smile. This was going to be an interesting night.

Chapter 11

Geoffrey took a long sip of his chardonnay. Tonight had been truly surprising. He had come to the little Italian place expecting to have a quiet night alone, but when he had spotted Maggie looking uncertainly around her as she sat alone at a table, he couldn't help but go over to her and invite himself to her dinner of one.

"You have a lovely smile, you know," Geoffrey said as he noticed Maggie watching him.

"Thank you," she answered in a somewhat uncertain manner.

"So, tell me, what do you do for a living?" Geoffrey asked, truly curious. He had asked Gillian a few times about her mother, but they didn't talk much, and the truth was he knew next to nothing about Maggie, something he would like to change.

"I write articles for a woman's magazine," Maggie answered, brushing a wisp of graying hair behind her ear.

The way her hair stuck out in odd places like it was rebelling against her orderliness made Geoffrey smile. It looked so charming on her.

"Well I would love to read one someday," Geoffrey said quickly.

"Really? I doubt you'd be interested in what I write about. Leonard never was." The bitterness burned in Maggie's voice and Geoffrey realized he had hit a sore nerve. "I- I'm sorry, I didn't mean to mention him. I just, we were together so long, you know?" she stammered, nervously scrunching her napkin in one of her hands.

"That's fine, I understand. Was Leonard your husband?" Geoffrey asked. He had heard she had been through a divorce but he hadn't heard anything about her husband, what he was like, or why they had separated. While he was curious, he reminded himself not to pry.

"He was until he decided to go looking for someone

younger," Maggie said, once and for all finishing off the poor napkin.

"Well, I know it won't necessarily make you feel better, but I do know what it's like to be separated from your spouse and not of your own choosing. I didn't mean to pry."

"I'm sorry," Maggie said softly. Somehow her being there made Geoffrey want to talk about what had happened.

"My wife walked out after twenty-five years together. Apparently, she needed to *find herself.* Sometimes I wonder if we would have had children if it would have changed something. Our marriage just fell apart over the years. I still loved her but things just got difficult." Geoffrey ran a hand through his hair in frustration. He didn't know how their conversation had turned to something so dismal.

"I'm really am sorry about everything. I feel so alone since the divorce, and if it weren't for Gillian I'd really be all alone," Maggie touched Geoffrey's hand as she spoke.

"To be honest, it's only now that I am on my own, I regret not having a family. My wife and I did everything together for the longest time. I suppose we found our family in each other instead of in children. But I'm an only child and my parents have passed so now that my wife is off somewhere finding herself, I suppose I feel like I really am alone, just waiting for myself to disappear as well." Geoffrey lowered his eyes and looked truly sad.

"Do you think she'll come back? Sometimes I think Leonard will come back. I expect to see him walk through the door with take-out and want to watch a movie together, but it never happens." Maggie looked forlornly outside the window for a moment.

Geoffrey felt his heart squeeze a little tighter as he heard Maggie's words. Those moments had happened to him more often than he would like to admit.

"You know, some days I really wish she would, and other days I just accept that this is the way it is now," Geoffrey sighed as he looked into Maggie's eyes. They sat there for several moments in silence just understanding each other.

He reached out and patted Maggie's hand, "Listen to us," he said as he placed his napkin carefully on his knee and moved his cutlery around. "I know there are a lot of regrets but I'm sure you will agree there were good times too." Geoffrey removed his hand and sat up a little straighter. He hadn't meant to push into Maggie's personal space. "Let's move on to lighter topics," he said with a little chuckle.

"I'm glad we got to talk a little about it, you know. It makes me feel like there's at least someone out there who understands. Even if your situation is a little different, it's still kind of the same," Maggie said in a rush that surprised Geoffrey. He nodded in agreement.

As they sat there, smiling at one another, the waiter appeared with their food and wine. Geoffrey didn't realize just how hungry he was until he started eating. Hardly a word passed between them while they savored the food, only speaking to comment on how delicious it was.

Geoffrey thought about what a wonderful surprise this had turned out to be. He rarely went out with friends as he tired of them asking if he'd heard from his wife, asking him if he was all right and what he was doing to occupy himself. Just because he was alone now, didn't mean that he no longer had a life. He looked over at Maggie, it was nice to spend some time with a kindred spirit like her.

They talked for hours after the meal. It was only when they looked around to see all the other tables empty and the waiters looking at them hopefully, that they realized how late it was.

"Shall we?" Geoffrey motioned toward the door.

"I think we'd better," agreed Maggie. "Before we get thrown out. I didn't realize it was so late."

"Did you come in a cab?" asked Geoffrey. "Would you like me to call one?"

"Oh no," Maggie said putting her jacket around her shoulders. "I only live around the corner. How about you?"

"Not quite just around the corner but a walk will do me

good." Geoffrey opened the door for Maggie. As he did, he waved to the waiters and called "Good night."

They both stepped onto the pavement. The night air was chilly, almost cold. Geoffrey smiled, maybe they would get a white Christmas after all. The recent warm weather they'd had was so uncharacteristic and everyone was hoping it would go away in time for their Christmases to be filled with snow.

"I'll walk you to your door," Geoffrey offered.

"That's very kind of you," Maggie said with a little smile.

They both set off down the road and Geoffrey hurried to follow Maggie's lead. They didn't speak but Geoffrey didn't feel as if it was an uncomfortable silence but a friendly one. It felt as if they had been friends for a very long time. Maggie stopped as they reached the main entrance to a large building.

It looked just like a place that Geoffrey would have imagined Maggie to live in; not quite as modern as everything else in town but certainly with its own elegant style that complimented Maggie's taste.

"Well, this is it," she said sounding a little disappointed, or was that just Geoffrey's hoping she was?

"Very nice," Geoffrey let his eyes wander up and down the building once more, committing its location to memory. He had seen it before but it had never had any specific significance in his mind until now.

They both stood looking at one another, the silence now becoming a little awkward. Maggie was the first to speak.

"I really enjoyed myself tonight," she said, her cheeks showing bright red in the light from the street lamp.

"Me too. Hopefully we'll do it again sometime," Geoffrey reached out and touched her shoulder a little in a sort of goodbye.

"Maybe," Maggie said almost in a playful tone as she turned to enter the building. "Goodnight, Geoffrey," she smiled over her shoulder and disappeared into brightly lit lobby beyond.

"Goodnight, Maggie," Geoffrey said softly, though he was

most certain she hadn't heard him.

He had made more than a friend tonight, he had made memories, and when you had as many bad memories as Geoffrey did, it didn't hurt to gather all the good ones he possibly could.

Chapter 12

Gillian smiled at the beautiful day, less than a month before Christmas and it still hadn't snowed a single flake. Despite most people waiting anxiously for snow, Gillian was actually glad that it was taking its time, she enjoyed all the extra sun she could get. Gillian's favorite days were days like these; cold but sunny, lovely for putting on your thick winter woollies and going for a walk. If she had the energy that is. She'd been up since five in the morning preparing for Geoffrey who'd promised to help her take the Christmas ornaments out of the attic cupboards so that she and the children could give them a good cleaning before the Christmas tree was delivered next week. She hadn't really believed Lorna about all the junk in the attic till she'd gone to find the ornaments. She made yet another mental note to do more attic cleaning when she got the chance. The children were so excited. Gillian had to force the older ones off to school with the promise that she wouldn't start on the ornaments till after dinner that evening. Kevin also said he would stop by on his way to the office, but it was already nine a.m. and neither of them had shown up. As Gillian went through the papers on her desk, she heard the front door open. She knew it was Geoffrey as soon as she heard the deep bass voice.

The office door opened, and Geoffrey put his hand around the door. He was holding one of those delicious coffee that Gillian loved, from the little shop on the corner.

"Sorry I'm late. Is it safe to come in?"

"Yes," Gillian gave a little laugh, "especially if that coffee is for me."

Geoffrey entered the office and put the coffee on the desk.

"Of course, who else would it be for?"

He sat down opposite Gillian as she greedily took the lid off the steaming coffee. She sat back in her chair and took a sip of the steaming hot liquid.

"Ah, lovely," she crooned almost to herself. "You seem to be in a good mood this morning. Something different?" It wasn't that Gillian saw Geoffrey all that often, but even so, he seemed a little different today, a little happier.

"No, nothing in particular. Life is good and all that." Gillian could tell Geoffrey was trying to sound nonchalant.

Gillian put the coffee down and leaned over the desk towards him.

"Come on, you know you can tell me all about it."

If Gillian didn't know better, she would have sworn that Geoffrey looked a little uncomfortable all of a sudden.

Geoffrey shuffled in his chair.

"I don't know how you'll feel about this, but actually I've quite enjoyed the company of your mother lately," Geoffrey finally said, surprising Gillian with his honesty.

Gillian gave him a side-ways look as she thought about the information. She had hoped that her mother and Geoffrey might get along when she'd invited her mother to take the children to go meet Santa.

"I don't mind Geoffrey, quite the contrary. Lorna and me were even discussing the possibility of the two of you getting to know each other,"

"Lorna and I," Geoffrey corrected. Maybe it was the fact that he'd worked as a grammar teacher for half of his career, or maybe it was just because he enjoyed reading, but he couldn't help but correct people when they used such poor grammar.

"I see, well I quite enjoy her company. She is a wonderful woman," Geoffrey said with a warm smile that nearly made Gillian giggle.

Geoffrey straightened in his chair. "What's funny?" he demanded.

"Just you, Geoffrey, you look like a little kid who discovered a new friend in kindergarten. I am really happy that you two are getting along. Mom has been pretty lonely since everything happened with Dad."

"How is your father by the way? You've never really mentioned him in the time I've known you," Geoffrey asked.

Gillian sighed sadly, "He still isn't answering my calls. I have no idea what's going on with him. I talked to him after the divorce and he seemed fine and then he just disappeared into thin air. Maybe he's starting to realize that Mom is really gone," Gillian said thoughtfully, for a moment, forgetting she was talking to Geoffrey and not to herself.

Before Geoffrey could answer, a loud commotion brought both of them to their feet and out to the hallway leading to the front door. Ray stood there nearly jumping up and down while a flustered Maggie took off her white fur coat.

Gillian tried to recover from the shock as she watched her mother place her umbrella in the rack beside the door. She couldn't remember a single other time that her mother had dropped in unannounced and she also couldn't remember how many times she wished that Maggie was the kind of mother to do that.

Now that it had happened, Gillian could hardly believe her eyes.

"Aunt Maggie, Aunt Maggie. Did you come to see me?" Ray was asking as he bounced around Aunt Maggie in circles before he flung his arms around her waist in a welcoming hug.

Gillian nearly laughed as her mother struggled to keep her balance but returned the boy's hug with an awkward one of her own and a smile.

"You're not the only person I came to see, but you are one of them!" Gillian heard her mother say. "Hang on, young man. Why aren't you at school?" Maggie's stern voice reminded Gillian of all the times her mother had asked her that same question. Gillian recognized the stern look on Maggie's face and Ray seemed to as well.

"I wasn't feel good this morning and so I got to stay home." Ray said proudly.

Gillian laughed out loud at this one, the way Ray said it, like he had won the lottery.

"You look like you're feeling better now. Do you have some reading books from school?" Maggie inquired.

Ray nodded. Gillian wasn't quite sure where this was going but decided to let it play out.

"In that case, once I get a chance to talk with my daughter, I will come through to the kitchen and we can have a reading lesson. You never know, you might learn something new and you do seem to be getting better by the minute."

Gillian giggled softly, suddenly realizing that her eyes were filling with tears. She missed this woman, this version of her mother who was kind and looking out for her when she was a little girl. She missed the mother who would sit and read with her for hours before bed so she wouldn't have nightmares, and it touched her heart to see that mom coming out for little Ray.

Raymond gave Maggie another hug, then he was tearing off towards his room, most likely to gather his reading books from school. Gillian wasn't sure when the last time was that she had seen him so excited.

Gillian hurried to greet her mother now that she was unoccupied.

"There you are Gillian," Maggie said, seeming a bit flustered. Gillian knew that her mother wouldn't have wanted her to witness her exchange with Ray, but she couldn't help watching.

"And Geoffrey, I'm sorry, I didn't know you'd be here this morning." Gillian watched as her mother's face turned deep red.

She looked between her mother and Geoffrey, something was obviously creating some tension in the room, she just wasn't sure what exactly.

"Mom, what are you doing here?" Gillian asked trying not to sound rude. There was nothing she appreciated more than her mother's unexpected presence and she hoped that she didn't sound ungrateful.

"Oh, I actually wanted to invite you to brunch a little later if you had the time," she said sheepishly. Gillian noticed her mother wringing her hands nervously.

"I'd love to Mom, thanks for thinking of me," Gillian said with a smile that she couldn't hold back.

"Well, I mean, I was going to eat anyway I just figured why not enjoy it together," Gillian's mother blushed even deeper as she avoided Gillian's gaze.

"Thanks Mom and thank you for spending a little time with Ray. It means the world to him," she added. Gillian reached out and gave her mother's arm a squeeze. She wanted to do so much more but decided she wouldn't embarrass her in front of Geoffrey.

"Let me know when you're done reading with Ray and I'll be ready to go," Gillian beamed.

"In that case, excuse me Geoffrey, excuse me Gillian, but I do believe I have a very eager young pupil waiting for me in the kitchen," Gillian's mother said with a twinkle in her eye.

"Go ahead Mom, and have fun," Gillian called after her.

She wasn't sure what had gotten into her mother lately, but she had to say she wouldn't change it for the world. Whoever this new woman was, Gillian actually felt like there might be a chance of rekindling a relationship with her once more and that would be the best Christmas present she could hope to receive.

Chapter 13

Maggie tossed her shoes off as she entered her apartment. It had been a long day and her entire body ached, but she wore a smile on her face. So much had happened in the last week. She had actually been spending real quality time with her daughter and she had developed a friendship with Geoffrey that she hadn't thought possible to find with someone again. And then there was sweet little Ray who beamed with happiness whenever she walked in the door.

The last week had been a jumble of visits at the orphanage, running with Geoffrey and keeping up with her writing deadlines in between. But she was happy. She loved feeling busy and she enjoyed feeling like she had a purpose in life besides just waiting for others to need her.

She hurried to the shower and closed her eyes as the hot water washed over her. Once again, her mind wandered to Leonard. Was this right? Was her life what it should be?

There were days when she found herself wishing there was a meeting to arrange or a luncheon to attend to and then she would remind herself that she hated that her life always revolved around him. In the end she would find herself so confused she didn't want to think about it anymore and then she tried her best to distract herself.

Soon she was settling down into bed. As she went through a checklist of things that were laid out for the next day, she tried to push the nagging thoughts of Geoffrey and Leonard out of her mind.

It was harder than she thought, and she soon found herself unsuccessful.

She pondered on Geoffrey, who had become her friend, but also had a wife whom she was sure Geoffrey hadn't come to terms with completely. The way he talked about her was the way she often thought about Leonard. She didn't blame him. It was only natural to miss someone you had spent half your life with, even if you had spent that half of your life asking why you were still with them.

She sighed, this all brought her to Leonard, good old Leonard. If he had come back to her begging for her forgiveness, she might have considered it, but in all the months it took to finalize the divorce and then the weeks after, he hadn't even called to see if she was okay.

Maggie wiped a stray tear from her eye,

"I can't afford to care," she whispered to herself in the dark.

The thing she hated most was the fact that it hurt her so much. All the nights she had spent rethinking the last several years, trying to remember what it was that had caused their marriage and their love to dissolve. It had happened gradually and there wasn't any specific event she could pinpoint, but the more she thought about it, the more she regretted the evenings when she'd been too tired to stay up to talk and the nights when feeling a little under the weather, she had ignored Leonard so she could have some time alone.

Maybe if she had made more of an effort…

"No, it wasn't all my fault! Some of it certainly was, but not all of it," she consoled herself.

Turning over she pulled the blankets a little closer to her chin. She needed to get some sleep and these memories were nothing if not depressing.

Determined to think of happier things, she pulled Gillian and Ray into her thoughts and smiled as she drifted off to sleep. Maybe half of her heart was stuck in the past but there was still a lot for her here in the present and in the future too.

---*---

Maggie balanced a box of fresh donuts under her arm as she approached the orphanage. She had heard Ray talking about donuts the other day and had been utterly astonished when he had said he couldn't remember the last time he'd had one.

She was determined to bring him some as soon as possible which turned out to be today.

She didn't ring the doorbell but walked right in, just the way Gillian had instructed her too. It felt odd not to be shown in, but it also felt satisfying in a way, like she belonged to the place.

She walked toward the front office, and opened the door confidently to find Geoffrey sitting at the desk opposite Gillian.

"Good morning Gillian," Maggie said lightheartedly.

"Geoffrey, I didn't expect to see you here," Maggie said, pleasantly surprised.

Gillian was busily writing down something on some sheets of paper in front of her.

"Oh, Geoffrey came by to help out a few hours this morning with the yardwork. I told him you might be stopping by, so he stuck around," Gillian explained with a little smile.

Geoffrey looked at Maggie sheepishly.

"I'm glad you showed up," he said. "I wondered if you were going to after all."

"Actually, Mom visits quite often now," Gillian spoke up, surprising Maggie.

"I used to hardly ever see her so I can't say I'm complaining," Gillian said with a little laugh.

"What's that supposed to mean?" Maggie asked indignantly. Then she turned to look at Geoffrey.

"It's not like I didn't want to visit before, I was just... busy." Maggie knew it wasn't a great excuse, but she had to try. "I brought the donuts I mentioned, are the children around?" Maggie tried not to appear too eager. She had changed a lot in the last couple of weeks and found herself enjoying the company of both the children and Gillian more than she would likely admit. She just wasn't sure how to embrace that change yet so she did what anyone did, tried to deny it was there at all.

"You seem to have quite the friendship with Ray. I'm glad. If anyone could use a little extra friendship, he could," Geoffrey said with a smile.

"He's a good kid, isn't he?" Maggie said with a smile of her own. I've been going through his reading books with him and he's made such improvement. I'm hoping these donuts will give him some encouragement today. Maggie paused, holding up the box of still warm goodies. "I'm going to go find Ray and a pot of coffee if I'm lucky. Feel free to join me. There's more than a dozen here," Maggie said with a laugh, showing the box of sugary treats once more.

It wasn't hard to find Ray. He was sitting patiently in the kitchen with two reading books in front of him. When Maggie sat down, she noticed the books looked more basic than the last ones they had read.

"Are these the books we're reading today?" she asked as she picked one up.

Ray flashed an embarrassed look in Maggie's direction.

"Yeah," he said, suddenly seeming discouraged.

"My teacher gave me these because she said I can't read properly," Raymond said, his head hanging a little lower.

"Oh, that's silly. You're a wonderful reader!" Maggie said lightly. "Tell you what, why don't you read through these fast so can go back to those harder books I know you're capable of reading."

Maggie lifted his chin gently.

"Pretty soon, you'll be reading chapter books, all by yourself!" Maggie exclaimed with a smile.

"Really?" Raymond asked excitedly.

"Of course. Even if I have to come every day and practice with you."

"Will you really come every day?" Ray asked a doubtful glint in his eye.

Maggie laughed and ruffled his hair, "I will certainly do my best," she said truthfully, after all, that was all anyone could do.

"I almost forgot! I have something in this box that I am sure will give you reading super powers," Maggie said with a laugh as she opened the lid of the donut box.

Ray squealed in excitement, "Thank you Aunt Maggie! Thank you, thank you, thank you!" Maggie couldn't help but burst into laughter at Ray's display of joy.

Soon his cries of glee brought several others of the young children into the kitchen to find out what had brought about such a commotion. Only when all the children had a piece of doughnut in their hands and Ray was settled down munching his happily did Maggie open the first book and start their lesson.

It didn't take long for them to go through all of the books and just as Maggie had suspected, Ray was much better at reading than he was given credit for. After getting through a few pages of a more challenging book, Maggie decided that it was enough for the day. She found herself considering a visit to Raymond's school to have a chat with his teacher. After all, it didn't seem as if he had anyone else to look out for him.

"Are there any donuts left for us?" Geoffrey's voice caused Maggie and Ray to look up from their conversation and their almost-gone donuts.

"We may be able to find a crumb or two," Maggie said in a mischievous voice while Ray giggled.

Gillian and Geoffrey joined in with the laughter and soon the four of them were sitting together enjoying a nice conversation among friends. Maggie smiled. It had been a long time since she had felt at home with a group of friends. She had always felt like she had to put forth a false image and convince people she was something she wasn't.

All too soon the donuts and coffee were finished, and the books were all put away.

As Maggie headed towards the door, she couldn't help but look back at the empty hall with a smile. In a way she had found what she had been missing here at the orphanage a place she had thought she would never enjoy. She couldn't have been more wrong.

Chapter 14

"My mom is going to be here any second," Gillian said nervously, pacing the kitchen floor. Kevin walked over to her in a few of his large strides, and stood in front of her, rubbing his hands up and down her arms in a quick invigorating motion.

"You told me that things have been going great with your mom," Kevin said encouragingly.

Gillian stared up into his eyes, trying to steal a little bit of his confidence.

"I know, I know. She has been great. She's been visiting the kids and me and making me feel… well like I have a mom again. It's just… I hope that she won't freak out. She hasn't even met you," she sighed.

Gillian hoped that her fears had no base in reality. For all she knew her mother would welcome Kevin into the family with open arms, but all the uncertainty she had held for the past several years kept creeping up on her and putting doubts in her mind.

"No matter how your mother reacts, I am not going anywhere," Keven said patiently with a smile.

Gillian nodded and began pacing again as she heard the car in the driveway.

She had invited her mother out to lunch in order to meet someone. What her mother didn't know was that it was her fiancée she was coming to meet, and she hoped their surprise wouldn't change all the progress they had made over the past few weeks.

Gillian really wanted to have a happy Christmas with her mother and the children, but she also wanted Kevin there and she didn't want to be hiding their relationship the entire time. It was past time that her mother knew she was getting married.

"Okay, okay, we can do this," Gillian said, plastering a smile she wasn't sure was real on her face. Her palms felt sweaty and she felt unsure of everything, but especially this luncheon with her mother.

Kevin took her elbow, providing a little bit of support that kept Gillian from teetering. Gillian felt that feeling a person feels when they jump off the edge of the swimming pool and they realize they're not ready but know they're about to hit the cold water at any moment.

As soon as Gillian's mother stepped from the taxi, she could tell that her mother noticed something was different.

Gillian had the urge to pull her arm away from Kevin's, but she forced herself to let it stay put.

"Gillian! It's so good to see you. And who is this?" Gillian could tell by her mother's tone that she was strained and struggling not to bombard her with questions.

"Mom, I want you to meet Kevin. We have actually been together for quite a while and I thought it was time the two of you got to know each other." Gillian smiled as she said all of this.

She figured she would tell her mother they were dating before they got to the restaurant and once they were there they would tell her they were getting married. After all, they didn't want to freak her out completely all at once.

"It's wonderful to meet you, Kevin." Gillian watched as her mother shook Kevin's hand with genuine interest.

"It's nice to finally meet you too," Kevin said gallantly as he returned her handshake.

Gillian kept her smile on her face while they all piled into the taxi. Maybe this wasn't such a bad idea.

---*---

Maggie couldn't help but keep glancing up at Kevin and Gillian as she ate lunch. They seemed happy and to have so many inside jokes they had to have been together for quite some time. Her emotions flip flopped from being offended that they hadn't told her sooner to being happy that Gillian had finally told her.

"So, Mom, now that you've met Kevin, we actually have some more news for you," Gillian said when they were enjoying cake and coffee.

Maggie looked up suddenly worried, "Are you pregnant?" she asked a million different things running through her mind.

"No! Mom, I'm not pregnant," Gillian looked at Kevin with her nervous look that Maggie knew so well.

"Actually, Kevin and I are planning on getting married," Gillian said with a big smile.

"Married?" Maggie parroted. She wasn't able to think of anything else to say at that moment. She wasn't mad exactly, but she was definitely not as fond of Kevin as she had been a few moments ago.

"I- you were just dating a few moments ago," she said trying to lighten the mood while she got ahold of her thoughts.

"I know, I should have told you sooner. It's just everything with Dad that was going on and then the divorce; I just thought it wasn't the right time. But in the last couple of weeks that we've been visiting more, well I just wanted you to know," Gillian explained.

Maggie looked at Kevin and then at Gillian. They certainly looked happy, and she could tell by the stubborn look on Gillian's face that if she weren't to approve it wasn't as if they were asking permission.

"Well, congratulations then. When's the wedding?" she asked tightly.

Gillian breathed out a sigh, "We haven't exactly set a date, but we are engaged," Gillian said with a little laugh.

"I would love to help you plan your perfect day," Maggie said lifting her coffee for another sip.

This new news would take a little getting used to, but she knew she would, in the end, have to be okay with it.

As long as Gillian was happy, that was what mattered Maggie told herself. She felt a little sad, hearing her daughter talk about her dream dress and the chapel she wanted the ceremony to be at. How had her daughter grown up so fast? What happened to the toddler who was learning the difference between her shoes and food?

Time had gone by so fast, and it hadn't really hit Maggie how grown up Gillian truly was until this moment. Of course, she had always known this day would come, but now that it was here it was hitting her a little harder. Maybe it just made her feel older.

Maggie smiled and laughed through the rest of lunch, but she knew it would be a lonely night at her apartment. She was truly happy for Gillian and she knew the time had come to let go of her baby girl.

Chapter 15

Geoffrey paced back and forth, re-reading the letter in his hand over and over. His wife had written him, and more than a few lines this time. She told of her recent trip and how she missed him and had been thinking of what they'd lost together.

"You mean what you lost," he mumbled angrily as he read that part of the letter once more. She didn't outright ask him to meet her, but he knew her. She was waiting for him to reach out to her. He couldn't do it, at least not yet. How could he? His mind turned towards Maggie. He had only known her for a few weeks, but he had some sort of feelings for her. Was it really love? He wasn't sure, and he definitely wasn't sure she was looking for that type of a relationship with him. There were times when he saw that far off look in her eye; the look he knew well of missing her ex-husband.

Going through a divorce or a separation wasn't as easy as it sounded. You didn't just forget everything you'd been through with that person. It didn't just go away. If anything, it was there stronger than ever as you remembered every good moment and tried to bring it back. It was there when you remembered every bad moment and tried to blame it on the other person.

Geoffrey sighed and laid the letter down on the countertop. He didn't have to answer her right now. He would think about it.

There had been a day when he would have jumped at the chance to have her back, when he would have gone and helped her pack to come home, but he wasn't sure how he felt about her anymore.

What he was sure about was that he enjoyed spending time with Maggie, even if it was just as friends. He put on his coat and grabbed his keys. He was going to be late for dinner at the orphanage.

As he drove, he cranked up the music as high as it would go. He needed some distraction for a little while, and an outing at the orphanage would do just perfectly.

Maggie paced back and forth in the large living room at the orphanage, she had something she needed to discuss with Gillian, and she was a little nervous about it.

"Okay Mom, all the kiddos are in bed. What did you want to talk about?"

"Should we leave?" Geoffrey's voice pulled Maggie's attention to where he was sitting beside Kevin.

"No, no, it's fine for you to stay. You'll all hear soon enough," she said, waving her hand in the air and trying to gather her thoughts. Maggie turned her attention back to Gillian, "I wanted to talk to you about Ray," she said, twisting her hands a little.

"What about him? Did he do something?" Gillian's eyes filled with concern.

"No, no, nothing like that. Actually I wanted to know what the possibilities are of adopting him," Maggie said in a rush.

She instantly saw the complete surprise on Gillian, Kevin and Geoffrey's faces.

"He's getting older and he still doesn't have a family. As much as I love reading stories with him and taking him to outings, I would love even more to give him the family he wants so badly," Maggie explained tears coming to her eyes.

She hadn't meant to become emotional, but it was happening against her wishes.

"Mom, I don't know what to say. I mean, I never thought you were the type to adopt," Gillian said, looking over at Kevin with an unreadable look.

"I know, I know, but there's something about Ray, and I know it's probably wrong, but I've grown to love him during the time we've spent together, and it breaks my heart that he thinks no one wants him." Maggie tried to explain her feelings.

"I think it's a splendid idea," Geoffrey finally said.

"You know what? Me too," Kevin chimed in. "If anyone deserves a home after so much time it's Ray,"

They all turned to Gillian.

"I think it's a good idea too as long as you are sure," Gillian said sternly.

Maggie couldn't blame her, after all she was in charge of these children and it was her responsibility to find good homes for them.

"I am absolutely positive. Where do we start?" Maggie said with enthusiasm.

"It's not that simple," Gillian laughed. "But we will start the process right away. You'll have to have home studies and fill out paperwork and the whole thing, but it's doable," Gillian laughed.

"He will be overjoyed when he hears," she said with a little giggle that reminded Maggie of when she was a little girl.

"I don't want to tell him just yet. I want to be sure that it is a done deal before I get his hopes up," Maggie warned everyone.

"Let's get the paperwork done as soon as possible so that we can tell him," Gillian said, now beaming with a smile that stretched from ear to ear. "This really is going to be a wonderful Christmas!"

Chapter 16

Maggie laughed and joined in with Gillian singing the lyrics to "We wish you a Merry Christmas." She couldn't be happier that Gillian had agreed to go Christmas shopping with her. Tomorrow was Christmas Eve and this morning they had all woken up to their utter happiness to more than four inches of snow.

Maggie glanced back at Ray who was happily singing along while clutching his Wendy's cup in one hand the remnants of a chocolate frosty in the other. It was looking pretty close to a done deal that Ray would be coming to live with Maggie, but Maggie still hadn't told him. She didn't want to get his hopes up in case it didn't work out, and she knew things like that could always fall through when you least expected it.

"I didn't remember how challenging it is to drive in the snow," Gillian said as the song came to an end. Maggie felt a slight grip of concern as Gillian leaned forward in her seat, straining to see in front of them.

It had started snowing harder since they had left the mall and dusk had turned into dark faster than they had expected.

The sound of a cellphone ringing filled the car and Gillian fished it out from the cup holder while keeping her eyes on the road.

"Gillian are you sure you should-" Maggie wasn't able to finish her sentence as she was interrupted by a thundering crash. Metal screeched as Maggie and everything around her was thrown into the air.

The sound of Gillian and Ray and herself screaming filled Maggie's ears, while all she could make out was snow and cracked glass and headlights. She couldn't tell where they were or what had happened. The snow swirled around the car and it seemed they were moving in slow motion. She was sure it must have only taken a few seconds for everything to settle down to silence, but it felt as if it were hours, or even worse as if time stood still as their car shook them like insects in a can.

When the silence finally came, Maggie wondered if the noise

hadn't been better. She could hear a slight ringing in her ears and a bright light blinded her. At first, she considered she might be dying, but after a moment, she realized it was the other car, flipped on its side, its headlights shining into her face.

"Gillian? Ray?" Maggie could hardly recognize her voice. It was shaky and full of fear.

Ray's crying was what she heard next. It started out as a whimper but soon turned to wailing.

"Ray, I need you to calm down," she said trying to make her voice sound more authoritative.

"Does it hurt anywhere? Are you bleeding anywhere?" Maggie reached up and tried to click the lights in the van on, but they didn't respond. Something must have gotten messed up in the crash.

She undid her seatbelt and stepped outside on shaky legs. The cold snow made her shiver harder than she already was.

She found herself grateful that the car had landed upright once it had finished with its spinning. If it hadn't, she wasn't sure what she would have done.

It took a few moments to get Ray's door open, but soon it wiggled loose.

Ray was already out of his seatbelt and waiting for her, jumping into her arms and wrapping them around her neck as he continued to sniffle.

"Are you okay? Stand up here on the snow," she demanded sternly.

She forced her almost numb fingers to work and pull out her cellphone. It was one of the only times she had ever needed the little flashlight feature. With the thin beam of light, she quickly but carefully went over Ray. Once she was certain that he was okay, she zipped his jacket and pointed towards a couple of trees that were a few feet away.

"Go wait under the trees. Stay there until I call you, okay?" she instructed urgently.

Ray nodded without question and moved to obey.

For a moment Maggie watched him before she rushed around

the car to the driver's side. Gillian hadn't said a single word in the entire time Maggie had checked on Ray and panic was now filling Maggie. She fought to control it as she took in the sight of the driver's door.

It was pushed in from the side. Whoever had hit them must have hit them from the side and not straight on, that was good at least.

Maggie tried to open the door to no avail. After a few moments, she ran back around the car and crawled through the passenger's side.

"Gillian, answer me! Please wake up!" she cried as she patted her daughter's shoulder. Maggie was shaking from the cold now and could barely hold her cellphone flashlight steady.

She breathed a momentary sigh of relief as she saw Gillian's chest rising and falling steadily.

She looked down at her cellphone, she needed to call someone. She opened the contacts list to find a single name, "Gillian."

Why hadn't she put more contacts into her phone? She just hadn't used it to call anyone else.

Maggie felt tears welling up in her eyes as a number popped into mind.

Her fingers began moving without waiting for her approval and the next thing she knew, she was listening anxiously to the tones coming through the line.

On the second tone, a familiar voice answered.

"Hello? Maggie?"

Maggie paused and her heart beat a little faster, suddenly she felt safe, just hearing his voice. She knew he would figure out what to do. "Leonard, we've been in a car accident," she said frantically.

"Maggie, okay, calm down, first I need you to hang up while I call 911, okay?" Leonard's voice was calm, in control, just like Maggie remembered it.

"Okay," she sobbed wiping away a tear from her eye.

"Where are you exactly?" Leonard said through the phone.

Maggie explained the best she could where they were and told him about the other car and how Gillian wasn't conscious.

She could hear the fear in his voice that reflected her own. While neither of them had been the perfect parents, there was one thing that meant the world to them, "Gillian."

She jumped when her phone rang again.

"I've called 911. They'll be there soon, and so will I. I'm on my way already. Just stay put and don't try to move Gillian. Keep warm. It's freezing outside." The sound of Leonard's voice began to calm Maggie's frantic pulse and heart.

She let herself listen to him and follow his instructions. She couldn't think right now, she just needed to obey someone else.

She looked at Gillian's pale face once more before heading out to join Ray.

She didn't want him near the other cars in case one of them started on fire or something. She also didn't want him to see Gillian if she were to…

No, she couldn't even finish that thought.

The severity of the situation hit her.

"Leonard, what if she's not okay? What if she doesn't wake up?" she asked in a near whisper, as she reached Ray.

"Don't think like that Maggie. You can't think like that. She's going to be fine. You're all going to be fine. I'm going to be there in one minute."

Maggie began to cry into the phone. She couldn't bear to lose Gillian, she just couldn't. She pulled Ray into her arms. He was trembling violently and clutched her in fear.

Everything else seemed to fade away, her worries about Kevin and Gillian getting married, the process of adopting Ray, her anger and hate for Leonard, her friendship with Geoffrey. None of it mattered at this moment. All that mattered was her daughter's life.

A battered red truck pulled up to the crash, screeching as it came to a stop. Maggie pushed Ray in front of her and they stumbled toward it.

"I'm here," Leonard's voice said through the little speaker

that Maggie was still clutching to her ear. When they reached the truck, Maggie came to a halt. The man standing in front of her resembled Leonard, but he wasn't the same as the last time she had seen him.

His face was gaunt and looked pained in some way. His clothes were a little too big for his body, or maybe he had lost a lot of weight. He had a beard and a mustache, something he had never allowed when they had been married.

He rushed toward her and motioned for Ray to get into the truck. He helped him climb in and turned the heat on full-blast.

"You wait inside little man. You'll catch your death out here," he said gruffly as he closed the door.

Maggie was still unable to take her eyes off him as he came back to her side.

"Where's Gillian?" Leonard asked, his eyes bouncing from one car to the other.

"Th- this way," Maggie stuttered as she led the way.

The sound of sirens and engines filled the air around them and soon they were surrounded by ambulances and paramedics and police. The flashing lights made the night seem surreal and nightmarish.

Maggie wasn't sure how she felt about seeing Leonard again. She had expected to feel repulsion and hate the way she had when she had found out about the affair, but instead, she just felt sad and sort of numb. She wasn't sure what to think. Questions filled her mind. What had happened to Leonard since the last time they'd seen each other. Why was he so…different?

As she watched the paramedics load her daughter into the ambulance, she knew her questions would have to wait. Right now, all that mattered was making sure their daughter was safe.

Chapter 17

Maggie jerked awake, she had started to fall asleep once more. It had been nearly four hours sitting on the small hospital bench outside intensive care and there was still no news on her daughter. She tried to think of it as a good thing. At least that meant they were still working on her, right?

Geoffrey had come to pick up Ray and take him back to the orphanage a little after the accident, and after sitting beside her awkwardly for the evening, Leonard had disappeared. Maggie peeked down the aisle. He had been gone for nearly ten minutes now. She wondered where he had gone. He wouldn't have gone home without telling her, would he? The thought made her feel nervous and she tried to push the feeling away.

Leonard could do what he wanted. They weren't together anymore. He didn't have any obligation to stay here with her if he didn't want to.

The thought of her daughter and what condition she might be in brought a fresh wave of emotion over Maggie and she struggled not to burst into tears. All the stress and fear of the evening was catching up to her and it felt as if it were going to drown her under its weight.

She put her face into her hands and rested her elbows on her knees, she didn't know how she was going to get through this if… No, she couldn't go there.

"Maggie? Are you all right? I brought you some coffee." a kind voice that Maggie hardly recognized said as a warm hand touched her shoulder.

Maggie looked up into Leonard's tired eyes, then at the outstretched coffee in his hand. She felt something break inside of her. Who was this Leonard? Was he really the same man she had been married to all those years?

The Leonard who asked if she was all right and brought her

coffee had disappeared soon after they were married, replaced with a version of him that was so engrossed with work and what others thought that he rarely remembered what she liked, or cared.

"Th- thank you," Maggie stumbled over her words, still trying to wrap her mind around the change.

Leonard nodded before taking up his seat on the bench, leaving a generous space between them, and picked up his coffee which Maggie assumed he had left there before bringing hers there.

They both sipped their coffee in silence, not saying anything for several moments.

"How have you been?" Leonard finally asked, looking over with something that Maggie would have sworn looked like concern.

"I've been good and visiting Gillian at the orphanage. Tonight, we were going Christmas shopping-" Maggie's voice broke as she remembered the happiness that had come before tragedy. She looked hard at her coffee trying to regain her composure.

"I'm sorry this happened, but it'll be all right. I'm sure they'll have some news soon," Leonard said in a voice that reassured Maggie more than it should have.

"I should have answered the phone." His words were spoken so quietly that they were nearly lost.

"What do you mean?" Maggie had heard that Gillian was having a hard time getting a hold of Leonard, but she had figured she had finally managed to talk to him, since Gillian hadn't said anything else about it.

"I stopped answering my phone. I just didn't want... couldn't talk to anyone. It wasn't Gillian's fault, but I'm sure she was hurt that she couldn't reach me," Leonard explained with a wave of his hand in a helpless gesture.

"You answered my call," Maggie said, the question lingering in her voice.

Leonard looked up and his eyes met hers. Maggie was surprised to find them full of sadness.

"I answered because it was you," he said before turning back to his coffee.

"What happened to you Leonard? Where's Carolyn?" Maggie hated to ask, but she had to. She couldn't live with the questions that were tumbling through her head and she knew that at least it would distract her from their situation for a while.

"She- we split up actually two weeks after you and I did," Leonard's voice was filled with an emotion that Maggie had never thought she would hear, regret.

"You mean, before the divorce? You weren't even together with-" Maggie paused to think about it a moment. "Why didn't you tell me?" she asked softly. At this point, what had happened didn't matter. What mattered was that it had happened in the first place and now she needed to understand why. Why hadn't Leonard fought for her when he had stopped the very thing that had ripped them apart in the first place?

"I wanted to. I mean, if it would have made you feel better, I would have told you, but I didn't want you to stay with me, in our marriage." Leonard looked away and Maggie could no longer see his face.

"Was being married to me really that bad?" she asked, her voice wavering slightly. Somehow, despite everything, she had thought that there had been something there, something good that had been worth it. Hearing that Leonard didn't feel that way nearly broke her heart all over again.

"No, that's not what I meant. I just wanted you to be happy, Maggie, and I didn't make you happy." Leonard turned to look at her, his eyes glistening with tears, startling Maggie more than any of his other behavior had this evening. She had only seen Leonard cry two times in his life; once had been at his mother's funeral and the other when their family dog of fourteen years had cancer and had to be put down.

"I don't understand. If you would have told me, maybe I wouldn't have left. Maybe I could have forgiven you." She wiped a tear from the corner of her eye quickly.

"I know Maggie. You were the least selfish person I've known my entire life. When you walked out that door, I realized what I had done, what I threw away and there was nothing I wanted more than to go running after you and beg you to give me another chance." Leonard's voice was filled with emotion and Maggie could feel her heart constricting. Everything she had thought about Leonard had been wrong, or had it? He had still had an affair. None of this changed that.

"Mr. and Mrs. Faulkner?" A doctor in a pristine white coat seemed to have appeared out of nowhere. He stood in the empty hall with a clipboard in his hand.

Leonard cleared his throat and stood up and Maggie jumped to join him.

"How is she? Is she going to be all right?" Maggie asked urgently. She tried to continue to breathe as she waited for the doctor's answer.

"She was hurt pretty bad. We're still waiting to see what's going to happen. We had to sedate her. Once the sedatives wear off, she may wake up or there's a slight possibility she could be in a coma. Her brain activity and vitals are stable at the moment, so we are hopeful that she'll pull through," the doctor said with a small plastic smile.

Maggie nodded and she followed close at his heels. She glanced back to make sure Leonard was coming as well.

The quiet rhythmical beep of the machines was unnerving to Maggie. She'd never liked hospitals much, and this was no exception.

Gillian lay on the hospital bed, her head wrapped in gauze bandages. She had several tubes hooked up to her and tape everywhere, but all that mattered to Maggie was that she was breathing and she looked almost comfortable.

Maggie took Gillian's hand gently in hers.

"I don't know if you can hear me, but I just want you to know how much I love you and I'll be here waiting for you when you wake up," Maggie said gently. She rubbed her thumb back and forth over the back of her daughter's hand. She noticed that her engagement ring had been removed. The hospital must have taken it off for the surgery.

"I know I was never the mother you deserved Gillian, but I hope you'll continue to give me another chance when..." Maggie couldn't say anymore, her shoulders began to shake as tears rolled down her cheeks.

Strong arms came out and turned her away from Gillian and Maggie sank into them. She let Leonard hold her as she cried for her daughter and for every mistake she'd made in life up to this moment. She had never realized the true importance of her relationship with her daughter and with Leonard until this moment and seeing the truth all at once was tearing her apart.

Chapter 18

Leonard watched Maggie as she slept in the recliner. She had fallen asleep after they had paced the halls for the past three hours. Finally, after numerous requests they had given them permission to sit in the room and watch over Gillian.

He traced the wrinkles on her face with his eyes, remembering the day when he had first seen her. She had been the spark of life in that internship. She had been the go-to girl and Leonard had seen her almost as a conquest.

He shook his head as he thought of his younger self. If only he had known what he knew now, things would be different. He would have treasured Maggie for the person she was.

As he watched her breathe in and out, he thought of everything that had happened, how they had gotten to this moment.

He hadn't meant to have an affair with the secretary. Maggie had been so busy and so had he. Slowly their marriage had developed a rift and the larger it became the less he knew what to do about it, so he did nothing.

Extra hours in the afternoons became late nights and one thing led to another. Carolyn had always made herself available. He should have seen that, seen the way she had looked at him. But he had been too focused on hating everything that bothered him about Maggie, and soon, things in the office weren't looking too bad.

He thought back to the first time. He had just had an argument with Maggie and decided to go to work. He hadn't known that Carolyn would be there, and when she was, they had started talking. It hadn't taken long for one thing to lead to the next. She had invited him to her apartment for lunch. They had had a few drinks.

"Don't you know it was wrong? How could you break us apart like this?" The memory of Maggie yelling at him when she had found out made him wince.

Of course, he had known it was wrong, but he'd figured that one time wouldn't hurt, after all, who would know? But one time had turned into more.

Leonard shook his head and walked over to stand by Gillian's bedside.

She hadn't deserved what he'd done. She deserved so much better, so much more. He stroked her hair back from her forehead. This was not what their family should be like, what they should be doing on Christmas Eve. Leonard checked his watch, it was nearly seven in the morning.

He smiled at the memory of Gillian running down the stairs at this hour, when she had been nine or ten, so eager to see what was waiting under the tree for her from Santa.

Of course, Leonard had never bothered with those sorts of things, but Maggie would always put something under the tree for Gillian with his name on it.

He chuckled softly as he remembered being almost as eager to see what he had gotten for Gillian as his daughter was. It was small things like that that he missed the most. Things that he had taken for granted all those years.

Maggie would have prepared a huge Christmas dinner tonight and their close friends would have come. If Gillian had someone special, maybe he would have come too. The vision of the happy family filled his mind and made his eyes sting once more. He wasn't a man to easily show his emotions, but lately, the things he thought of hit so close to his heart it was hard not to express his sadness.

"Is everything all right?" Maggie's tired voice wafted over to him, interrupting his remembrances.

"Yes, I was just thinking about what we would be doing right now if this hadn't happened, if none of it had happened," Leonard said softly.

"Why didn't you come after me Leonard?" Maggie looked up at him with eyes full of questions.

Leonard's heart beat faster and all the doubts and fears of

rejection filled him. How could he have asked that of her? The one person who had stood by him through everything, the one he had betrayed.

"I didn't want to hurt you anymore…" Leonard paused, "And I figured that if I couldn't forgive myself for what I did, that I couldn't possibly ask you to forgive me," Leonard finished with a sigh.

"You should have let me make that decision Leonard." Maggie's voice was stern and almost made Leonard smile. He missed her. He missed every one of her moods and scoldings and he even missed fighting with her. There was nothing like losing what you had to realize what it was worth having.

"What did you do all this time? You didn't even show up for the court hearing for the divorce to contest the papers." Maggie said it almost as a thought to herself rather than a question.

"You deserved everything you asked for. I wasn't about to stand in your way. I actually went on a trip to Mexico," he said quietly.

"To Mexico?" Maggie squeaked. Leonard could see the fear in her eyes. They had always heard bad things about Mexico. It had been one of the reasons that he had gone. He had wanted to feel like he was doing some good in the world for once. The experience he had found with the orphans in Mexico had been like nothing else he had ever done. He had come to appreciate simple things that he had long forgotten even existed.

"I miss you," she said simply.

The words surprised Leonard making his head snap around to look at Maggie.

"Why? All I ever did was hurt you. How could you miss that?" he asked, a sense of awe coming over him.

"There were good times too, but I am not sure if I'm ready to forgive you," she said.

Leonard watched as a range of emotions played over Maggie's face. He wondered what she was thinking at this moment.

Suddenly, movement caused Maggie to leap from her chair and join Leonard at the side of Gillian's bed.

"Is she waking up? Gillian honey, can you hear us?" Maggie stroked Gillian's hand and Leonard watched anxiously for any more movement. She had moved her hand, not a lot but just enough.

After a few moments of holding their breath silently, Gillian's eyes began to flutter slightly, and the next thing Leonard knew she was looking up at him.

She moved her mouth open and closed as if she were trying to say something, but no sound came out.

"Don't talk, we'll get the doctor, just rest," Leonard said quickly before rushing from the room. He came back with a doctor in tow who brought a small cup of water for Gillian.

After she'd taken a few sips the doctor pushed some buttons on the bed to adjust her position.

"Look at you guys, bickering like an old married couple," Gillian croaked out softly after she had been attended to.

Leonard and Maggie both laughed.

"You heard all of that?" Maggie asked, her cheeks blushing a deep red.

"No not all of it, but enough," Gillian said as she went into a fit of coughing.

"You need to rest and try not to over exert yourself. You've gone through surgery and have been in a coma for the last twelve hours," the doctor said with a serious tone. He listened to her heart and took her blood pressure. He looked at Maggie and Leonard as if trying to decide whether he should allow them to stay or not.

"I'll be back to check on you in a bit. She needs to rest. Tomorrow she will be in her own room and you can return."

"Ok let us say our goodbyes," Maggie said. The doctor nodded and ducked out of the room.

Leonard watched as the man left their room and walked down the hall. He wondered if he was going to give good or bad news to another family today, on Christmas Eve.

"Where's Kevin?" Gillian asked, bringing Leonard's attention back to her.

"Who's Kevin?" Leonard hadn't heard of a Kevin and by the way Gillian was looking around the room for him with big eyes, he suspected that he was something more than a friend.

"Oh, I forgot you didn't hear, Kevin is my fiancée," Gillian said with a shy smile.

Leonard gave a tight smile, he knew he didn't have any say in the matter, but it was still hard to see his baby girl growing up.

"I think he's in the waiting room, he came by a little earlier and I told him we'd let him know if your condition changed," Maggie said, patting Gillian's hand lightly.

"I'll go meet him and give him an update. After all it seems we have to have a little dad to son in law talk," Leonard said with a good-hearted wink.

The last thing he heard as he left the room was Gillian's annoyed sigh and hurried instructions not to embarrass her. Leonard smiled as he headed towards the waiting room. Slowly the darkness from the last night was lifting and it couldn't have felt better.

Chapter 19

Gillian was sitting up in bed when Maggie arrived at the hospital first thing in the morning. She had waited impatiently for visiting hours to begin. She was glad they had moved her out of intensive care to her own room. That meant she was going to be ok and that was a huge relief.

"Mom, what's going on with Dad? Is he okay?" Gillian looked up at Maggie with concerned eyes. Maggie could tell Gillian had the same worries that had crossed Maggie's mind earlier. She didn't want Gillian to worry though. While she was the happiest person alive about Gillian waking up, she still hated to see her so pale and hooked up to all the machines. It was a reminder that life was fragile, that bad things could happen to you or your family and Maggie had had enough bad things for one week.

"I don't know. He actually told me he and Carolyn broke up long before the divorce. I'm not sure what to think," Maggie confessed.

Gillian tilted her head to the side and looked up at Maggie with an almost comical expression.

"Do you still love him Mom?" she asked softly.

Maggie was caught off guard by the question.

"I don't know Gillian. After all, what is love?" she asked. It was something she'd found herself thinking about a lot lately. What was love and how did you truly know if you loved someone?

"I don't know how to put it into words Mom, it's more complicated than that," Gillian said with a little smile.

"Do you hate him?"

"No, I don't hate him, I mean- I don't really know what to think right now Gillian. I really don't," Maggie sighed and pulled the chair up to the side of the bed and sat down, taking Gillian's hand into hers once more.

"I think you should ask yourself, would you regret anything if he died tomorrow?" Gillian said softly, breaking the silence and monotony of the beeping machines once more.

The new question made Maggie's heart beat a little faster. The idea of Leonard dying brought tears to her eyes. All the lost moments, all the lost laughter, never having come to an understanding of what really had happened between them.

He hadn't been with Carolyn. He had gone to Mexico. The Leonard she'd known would have never stepped outside of his office had it not been necessary, much less gone to Mexico.

"I hope he's not going to cause the wedding to be put off," Gillian said with a little giggle after Maggie pondered in silence for several minutes.

"I doubt your father would do that, he probably just wants to get to know Kevin and I'm sure if he gives him a chance, he'll come to find what a wonderful young man Kevin is, just like I have," Maggie said with a grin.

"Aww, thank you, mom, that really means a lot to me. You being in our lives means a lot to us." Gillian winced as she reached up to wipe a tear from her eye and Maggie hurried to help her.

"You know, I don't say this often, but it's not because I don't mean it. It's just... well my relationship with your father isn't the only one I have neglected over the years." Maggie paused and tried to gather her emotions before continuing.

"I love you Gillian, and I'm sorry for everything I did wrong as a mother and for every time I wasn't there for you." The words were hard to say, but once they were out in the open Maggie felt a weight lift off her shoulders.

"It's okay Mom. You know, having you say that really makes up for a lot of things, and I love you too. It's okay to say it more often. We all need to hear it once in a while," Gillian said giving Maggie's hand a tight squeeze. Two more tears made their way down Gillian's cheeks and Maggie moved to wipe them away.

"I'd best go see where your father is. He said he would be here early and so did Kevin. Heaven forbid he actually does try to sabotage your wedding," Maggie said with a mischievous smile as she left the room dabbing her eyes. Somehow, despite the emotions inside her making her want to go and have a good cry, she couldn't help but feel like this was turning out to be a good Christmas after all.

"Oh!" Maggie cried out as she nearly tumbled into Leonard not a few steps from Gillian's door. He and Kevin were talking to each other as if they'd known each other for years. Leonard reached out to steady Maggie.

"Sorry, I hope I didn't take too long, we were just getting acquainted on the walk over," Leonard said with a grin, "I do have to say she didn't pick a bad one," Leonard said with a chuckle.

"Of course, she didn't. We raised her better than that," Maggie said playfully looking stern as Kevin squirmed under their gazes, looking most uncomfortable.

"I think I'll go in and say hi," Kevin said, ducking out of the conversation and walking quickly into Gillian's room.

Leonard and Maggie followed close behind but stayed outside the room as he went to say hello to their daughter. They were out of earshot, but Maggie was sure they were saying something loving as the two had the biggest grins possible on their faces.

"Young love…it still exists," Leonard said somberly.

"Remember when we were like that? We used to go to that little café over by the library and share the banana split." Maggie smiled at the memory of her and Leonard sitting at their table, dividing the banana split directly down the middle.

"I remember," Leonard said, turning to face her.

"Leonard, I don't know how to move forward from here, but I want to try," Maggie said, surprising herself. She had been thinking about the words and despite her doubts they felt right once they were out in the open. She saw a spark of hope in Leonard's eyes. Maybe he did care after all.

"You have no idea how much that means to me, Maggie."

Leonard reached out and took one of her hands in his sending an electrical tingle down Maggie's arm. She hadn't known it was possible to feel this way again, especially about Leonard.

"I am sure we will have plenty of conversations about the past, and you have a right to know anything you want to ask me, but I want you to know right here, right now, you are the loveliest caring woman in the world. And it would be an honor to get to know you again for who you really are. If that means we can just be friends or even just people who used to know each other and sometimes go have a banana split, that's okay with me." Leonard's eyes searched hers and Maggie held his gaze, letting his words wash over her.

"Thank you, Leonard. Let's just take it slow. There's a lot we don't know about each other, even though we were married for twenty-five years. I think we grew to be two different people. Maybe if we can get to know who those people are again, we'll have a chance… at something." Maggie smiled up at him. She took in the wrinkles around his eyes she knew so well and the crook of his smile.

This had been her husband once, and if there was something she'd realized tonight, it was that someone could disappear in the blink of an eye. No moment was promised. No day was a guarantee, and she wasn't about to pass up resolving the past and possibly even pursuing a future. Maybe she didn't know if she still loved Leonard, but she knew there was something there. She did still care about him in a very special way and that was something worth fighting for.

She turned her gaze back to Gillian through the window. She was looking at their joined hands with a funny little grin. Maggie grinned right back and let her hand stay where it was. Maybe they were here at this hospital for a reason, and maybe they were all discovering something about real love tonight. Maybe this Christmas wasn't so bad after all.

Chapter 20

Gillian laughed as she watched Geoffrey lift Ray up to see outside the hospital window. The hospital had been reluctant at first, but they had agreed that the children and her parents and friends could come by for a small Christmas celebration in her room. There were Christmas lights strung up and a tiny tree on the side table. Someone had even put a little mistletoe above the door way.

Geoffrey had put on Christmas carols playing from the speaker of his smartphone. Kevin sat near her bedside. He hadn't let go of her hand for more than a couple of seconds the entire afternoon.

"Everyone, I'd like to make a toast!" Leonard was standing near the foot of her bed, a wine glass filled with coke in his hand. They hadn't thought it would be good to bring real wine to the hospital, so someone had brought soda to have with their cake and cookies instead. The children from the orphanage stopped their chatter. Maggie and Lorna hurried to arrange them in a neat little group, all holding their foam cups of soda expectantly.

"I want to give thanks that my daughter is well after the accident she went through and that I am able to be here with my wonderful family and all of their friends. Here's to a Merry Christmas!" Leonard said raising his glass.

The children giggled as they copied him before trying to drink their soda as quickly as possible in hopes of receiving seconds.

Gillian watched as the chocolate cake decorated in Christmas colors was divided up onto the small party plates and a piece was passed to everyone. Her arm was feeling much better and she was able to accept her plate without any help.

She savored the first bite of her cake. It was delicious and her favorite flavor too. She felt kind of bad changing everyone's Christmas plans, but she couldn't complain. Yes, it was tiny and cramped and their Christmas tree wasn't bigger than a shoebox, but it was cheerful and the spirit of Christmas filled the room.

She watched as her father leaned in to say something and her mother burst into laughter. She looked over to see Geoffrey telling the kids a story about Santa and how hospitals were always his first stop because that's where people needed extra cheering up. He led them to a small medical closet where much to their delight he pulled out a large sack of presents, handing one to each child.

Gillian laughed as her mother and father realized they were under the mistletoe and her father bent down to give her mother a little kiss on the cheek. It was a start and Gillian hoped that they would be able to rekindle something between them; they had more in common and needed each other more than they realized.

Geoffrey handed his post as Santa Claus to Kevin as he received a phone call. When he came back in the room Gillian wasn't sure what to think.

"Who was it?" she asked, curiosity getting the best of her.

"My wife," Geoffrey said with a strange look. "She wants to meet for coffee."

"Are you going to go?" Gillian had heard about Geoffrey's troubles with his wife and she hoped this was a good thing.

Geoffrey stared over to where Leonard had his hand on Maggie's shoulder.

"Maybe I will. It's Christmas day after all," he said with a little smile. "Maybe coffee would be nice." He walked back over to Kevin and rejoined the excited children as they peppered him with questions.

Gillian couldn't keep the huge grin off her face. This was the best Christmas she'd had in a long time despite the headache. Even though there was still tension between some of them and their lives weren't perfect, this moment was perfect. Somehow, they were all here together, all the people she cared about most in the world, sharing a simple Christmas because they cared about her.

Gillian snuggled a little deeper into her pillows and took another bite of chocolate cake. This would be a Christmas she would never forget.

Sample Story

Sara in Montana by Morris Fenris, ASIN: B00GU2DJBO

Chapter 1

Sara pulled up in front of the small drug store and leaned her forehead against the steering wheel for a brief moment. She was somewhere in eastern Montana, not sure exactly where, but she had been driving for two days straight. She had seen the sign for the little town and pulled off the highway in desperation. She was hoping to find a place to hole up, for just one night.

Exhausted, she pushed herself back from the steering wheel, reached across the console for her purse and turned to open the door. The harsh winter wind rushed into the car as she pushed the door open. Shivering, she pulled her thin shirt around herself and carefully navigated the snow and ice until she reached the sidewalk. Thank goodness, someone had shoveled the surface. Her thin tennis shoes were no match for the snow and she could already feel the moisture seeping through.

Pulling the door open, she hurried inside and then paused. On any other day, she would have stopped to appreciate the Norman Rockwell-like scene before her. The sounds of Christmas music filled the air and the old-fashioned soda fountain was decorated with garlands and tiny Christmas lights. A tinsel Christmas tree stood atop the countertop and fake snow had been sprayed around the mirror which made up the bar's back wall. Black and white tiles and red vinyl booths completed the picture.

Christmas was still several weeks away but the festive atmosphere in the store just augmented Sara's situation. She should be baking cookies with her niece and fighting the crowds at the mall.

Instead, she was in the middle of nowhere and running out of options. Right now, her only goal was finding a restroom.

As she scanned the back of the store, looking for a sign that would direct her to their bathroom facilities, she was once again wracked by a coughing spell that had her holding her ribs and bending over at the waist in an attempt to control the pain. She had begun coughing yesterday morning, and the coughing fits had gotten so bad she had been forced to stop driving several times during the day.

Managing to get control of her breathing once again, she straightened and started to move forward, only to run into a wall of muscle. Quickly glancing up, she moved back as she looked into the bluest eyes she had ever seen.

"I'm sorry," she told the man in front of her, hoarsely. Swallowing, she tried to find her voice again, "I didn't see you there. Excuse me." Sara attempted to walk around the man only to find her path blocked as he moved with her.

"That cough sounds pretty nasty. Are you okay?" Trent Harding asked. He had been sitting at the counter talking to Jeb Matthews, the drugstore owner, when he had seen the strange vehicle pull up in front of the store.

As the town sheriff, Trent knew every vehicle the 1,356 residents of Castle Peaks, Montana drove. The silver Camry parked out front was not one of them.

"I'm fine," Sara replied, as she looked at her feet. Not quite meeting his eyes, she asked, "Um, is there a bathroom here I could use?" Thanks to her latest coughing fit, finding a bathroom was becoming her number one priority.

"Sure. Just go straight back. It's on your left," Trent gestured behind him.

Sara cut her eyes back to his briefly and just nodded. Edging around him, she quickly navigated her way through the aisles, finding the bathroom and closing herself inside.

Trent watched the small woman until she located the bathroom. His radar was on high alert as he took in her appearance. Wearing a thin button down shirt over a t-shirt, well-worn jeans, and tennis shoes that appeared to be wet from their encounter with the snow, she was completely under-dressed for a Montana winter.

Puzzled that someone would venture out into the weather like that, especially while they were sick, Trent turned back to look at the vehicle parked out front. The license plates showed the vehicle was registered in California. Making a mental note of the plate number, he turned and took his seat at the bar again.

"That little gal seems like she's not feeling so well. That's a pretty bad sounding cough," Jeb said, as he finished wiping down the counter.

"Yeah. Car's registered in California."

"California? She's a long way from home then."

Trent and Jeb both turned at the sound of the bathroom door opening and watched as the young woman headed back towards the front of the store. As she drew closer, Trent got a better look at her and could not help but smile in approval. She was only around 5' 6" tall, almost a foot shorter than his 6' 4" height, with gorgeous baby blue eyes framed by long lashes. Her complexion was blemished by the weather and her long blonde hair was pulled up into a haphazard ponytail that was slightly askew. Her clothing did nothing to hide the curves hidden underneath.

Coming around from behind the counter, Jeb wiped his hands on the towel at his waist and held his hand out as she approached him,

"Good afternoon, Jeb Matthews at your service. What can I help you with?"

Sara hesitantly shook the older gentleman's hand. He reminded her of her late Uncle Thomas. His white hair and friendly demeanor helped to put Sara at ease. Swallowing, Sara said, "Would you happen to have any cough medicine?" Coughing again, she held onto her ribs until the fit had passed. She felt light headed as the spell eased, and struggled to catch her breath.

Jeb watched the young woman start coughing again and hurried around the counter, returning with a bottle of water which he uncapped and pushed into her hands. "Drink some of this and see if it helps."

Sara took the water and drank several small sips before she felt able to talk once again. "Thank you."

"Let me show you where I keep the cold remedies and we'll see if there's something there that might help you with that cough." Jeb indicated that she should follow him with a nod of his head.

After looking at several shelves, he bent and retrieved several boxes of cough syrup. Handing them to Sara, "One of these should do the trick. Have you been running a fever?"

Sara took the boxes he held out to her, and pretending to look at the usage directions, she shrugged one shoulder, "I don't really know. Probably...I...um..." Sara handed the boxes back and once again wrapped her arms around herself. She needed her glasses. Without them, she could barely make out the large printed brand name, let alone read the smaller typed directions for how to use the medicine. They were in the car but she did not have the energy to go get them. It was only cough syrup. They were all alike, weren't they? Sara didn't really know. She couldn't ever remember being this sick. "Maybe you could just choose one for me?"

Something was off here, but Jeb couldn't quite figure out what. Chalking it up to her not feeling well, he turned to where Trent sat observing their interaction, "Hey, Trent, which one of these would you recommend for her cough?" Jeb held both boxes aloft so Trent could see them.

Trent stood up and walked over to look at the boxes himself. Sara glanced at him quickly and then looked away again. He was wearing a badge. How had she missed that the first time? That was the last thing she needed right now. She wasn't sure how far David Patterson's influence reached, but if he had California law enforcement on his side, God only knew whom else he could influence.

Reaching out and removing the first box of cough syrup from Jeb's hand, she told him, "I'm sure this one will be fine. If you could ring me up I'll be on my way."

Sara turned and started to head towards the checkout counter, only to find her way once again blocked by a wall of muscle. Looking up she found her gaze trapped in that of the sheriff. He was the most handsome man she had ever seen. Luxurious hair that just begged to have her fingers running through it framed a strong face. Eyes that made her think of the night sky and a mouth that made her stomach flip filled her vision. Glancing down, the vision only got better. His shirt did nothing to hide the sculpted muscles of his chest and arms. Blushing at where her eyes had been headed, she forced her eyes to discontinue their southern perusal. She raised her eyes back up to see him giving her the same visual inspection.

She was gorgeous. Trent watched as her eyes scanned his face and then traveled down his body. He quickly did his own appraisal and definitely liked what he saw. Glancing down at her ring finger, he was pleased to see it vacant. He wasn't sure whom she was in town to visit, but he hoped she would stick around long enough for him to get to know her a little better.

"Excuse me," Sara attempted to go around the sheriff again.

Again, he moved with her, stopping her forward motion. "My name's Trent Harding, and you are?" Trent held his hand out, and when she didn't seem inclined to take it, he slowly reached up and rubbed his forehead, considering her skittishness all the while.

"Just passing through." Sara didn't have it in her to stand and trade niceties with this man. He was definitely someone she would have enjoyed looking at in another life, but now she needed to pay for the cough syrup and find the highway again. There were still several hours until dark and she needed to find some place to hunker down for the night. She should probably fill up with gas before leaving so that she could keep the heater going throughout the night.

For the last several nights, Sara had found secluded rest spots and spent her nights sleeping for short periods before the cold would force her to start the car and run the heater. She hoped that one more night and another day of driving would place her far enough away from San Francisco that she could stop and finally get some much needed rest. She was more tired than she could ever remember being and the coughing spells took every ounce of spare energy she could muster. What she wouldn't give to curl up in a nice warm bed and sleep for the next 48 hours.

Trent's radar went on alert even more as she attempted to get around him again. Taking hold of her elbow, he felt her stiffen, but she didn't try to pull away. He turned her toward the register and together they walked towards it. Looking down at her, he tried again, "I still didn't catch your name."

Sara looked up at Trent, and licking her lips replied, "I'm Sara." Trent watched her tongue come out and wet her dry lips, then felt his body instantly respond. What was it about this woman? He'd never felt this instant attraction before.

"It's nice to meet you, Sara. I see your car is registered in California. That's quite a ways from here. Are you visiting family for the holidays up here?"

Sara shook her head, "No."

Jeb took the cough syrup from her and rang it up. "That'll be $10.83."

Sara swallowed and forced her sense of dread down. She had been very careful only to use cash since she started running, but that was mostly gone now. Seeing no other way to get what she needed, she asked, "Do you accept credit cards?"

"Sure we do." Sara handed her card over and then signed for the purchase. Now she really needed to get on the road again. She had no doubt in her mind that David and his goons would be monitoring her credit cards. Within hours they would know exactly where she was. Grabbing the bag that Jeb handed her, she turned and hurried towards the front door, coughing as she went.

Seeing her hurried attempt to leave the store, Jeb called after her, "Miss, don't you want your receipt?" When she didn't turn or respond, Jeb slowly put the receipt in the cash register drawer and watched her exit his store. Concern etched across his face. That little gal was sick and needed someone to look after her. With a raised eyebrow, he gave Trent a look and nodded his head towards the door.

Trent watched Sara stop on the sidewalk and double over when the coughing fit didn't immediately subside. That was one sick woman who had no business driving around right now. Deciding it was his civic duty to try and talk some sense into her, he went after her. As he stepped outside, he wished he had grabbed his jacket. A winter storm was headed their way, and the wind had been picking up all day long.

Sara hurt so badly she didn't know how she was going to be able to continue driving anymore. Taking shallow breaths to try and quell the most recent coughing spell, and shivering from the biting winds, she started towards the vehicle only to find her path blocked once again. What was it with this man? She didn't have the energy to deal with this right now.

"Ma'am, I really think you need to think about getting off the road for the night. You don't seem like you're in the best shape for driving on the highway."

Sara shook her head. She needed to leave town - now. "Sheriff, thanks for your concern, but I really need to be on my way."

"Where are you headed?" Something wasn't adding up and he could see Sara growing more agitated by the minute.

"I...I just need to get back on the highway. I'm running kinda late because I haven't been feeling well." Wrapping her arms around herself, she tried to shield herself from the ever-increasing wind and cold.

"Running late?" Trent could see her start to shiver, but was more interested in getting some answers. He was a good reader of people, and this little gal was definitely hiding something.

Sara nodded quickly, trying to think of something that would reassure the Sheriff and get him to leave her alone. Where was she again? Oh yeah, Montana. What did she know about Montana... Helena was the capital. Striving to keep her voice even and not give way to the lie she was about to tell, she looked Trent in the eyes as she told him, "I'm headed to Helena. My fiancé is flying in tomorrow and I'm supposed to pick him up at the airport so we can spend the holidays with his parents." Sara barely hid her nerves as she spun the tale.

"Helena, huh? You've still got several hours of driving left ahead of you. And there's another snowstorm supposed to start later this evening."

"That's okay. I've driven in the snow before. I'll be fine, but I would like to get back on the road." Sara's voice was only a whisper by this time. Her throat felt as if it was on fire, her head was throbbing, and her chest hurt if she tried to take a deep breath. Combine that with the biting wind and uncontrollable shivers that had taken over her body, and she knew her ability to continue on her journey was in danger of coming to an abrupt halt.

"Well, if you are sure." Trent moved a step back and opened the car door for her. Surreptitiously glancing inside the backseat, he saw a small duffel bag, along with several blankets and a pillow. It almost appeared as if she had been sleeping in her car.

Sara nodded and slid into the driver's seat. The cold wind had her teeth chattering and her hands were so cold, she wasn't sure if she could turn the key in the ignition. After fumbling to grasp the key for several moments, she finally caught hold of it and started the car. Turning towards the open door and the waiting Sheriff, she gave him a small smile and said, "Thank you for your help."

Trent returned her smile. "No problem. You drive safe now. Merry Christmas."

Sara was so cold; all she could do was give a slight nod in recognition of his well wishes. She did not have the energy to dwell on the upcoming holiday season and what might have been. Right now, her survival was the only thing she could focus on and that required her to keep pushing farther east.

Trent stepped back, closing her car door and watched as she put the car into gear and headed back towards the highway.

Try as she might, the sheriff's parting words stayed with Sara as she backed out and headed the car back towards the highway. It was supposed to have been a wonderful Christmas. She had looked forward to her first holiday season as a married woman, decorating a tree together for the first time with her husband, inviting their family and friends over for dinner. She mentally gave herself a shake. Those dreams were gone now. Any Christmas spirit she did have vanished along with her hopes and dreams of being happily married to the man of her dreams. Nightmares are what they had become.

Wanting to take her mind off her morose thoughts, she turned the radio back on and tried not to think about what might have been. The radio announcer had just finished his weather report and it wasn't sounding promising for her. They were expecting up to a foot of snow, and a travel advisory had just been issued for central Montana as the winds were supposed to kick up and blow snow across the highway known to be treacherous. Sara had never driven in the snow prior to this trip and had scared herself several times during early morning hours as her car skidded on the icy patches dotting the highway.

Sarah briefly thought about turning around and seeing if the small town had any type of hotel accommodations, but then she remembered having used her credit card to pay for the cough syrup. Anyone looking for her would be able to track her credit card use. She definitely needed to put some miles between herself and Castle Peaks, Montana. Another state or two between them would suit her just fine.

****

Rubbing his hands together, Trent quickly re-entered the drugstore, seeing Jeb standing at the front window watching her car drive away.

"You couldn't convince her to stay, huh?"

"No. She says she's headed to Helena to pick her fiancé up from the airport in the morning. I hope she beats the storm. I don't think that little car of hers was meant to handle a Montana blizzard."

"She doesn't look like she's ready for a Montana winter. That girl didn't even have a coat on."

Trent's radar was still going off. Something here just wasn't right. "Hey Jeb, let me see that credit card receipt she signed."

Jeb looked at Trent, wondering what was going through his head, but opened the drawer and took out the receipt. Glancing at her signature, he read, "Sara Brownell."

Trent took the offered receipt and a notepad from his pocket. Jotting down her license plate number, he added her name and then pocketed the pad and the pen. "I'm gonna go back over to the office and check a couple of things out real quick. I'll see you later on."

"You gonna run that girl through the system?" Jeb asked.

"I'm gonna go run the plates first. Make sure the vehicle's registered to her and that everything's in order."

Jeb nodded and said, "I hope you don't find that girl's in any trouble. I get the sense that she's had it pretty rough recently."

Trent didn't reply. He would reserve his comments until after he had some facts. His gut told him that she was in trouble; what sort, he aimed to find out.

Chapter 2

Sara had almost made it back to the highway when another coughing fit struck. This one was the worst yet and she had no choice but to pull off the side of the road and place her car into park. Holding her chest, she tried desperately to stop the coughing. Knowing there was no one around to see, she gave free rein to the tears that came with the agonizing pain. As the coughing fit stopped, she pushed the driver's seat back a little and pulled her knees up to her chest, trying to hold herself together.

Sara leaned her head back and closed her eyes, trying to take slow, calm breaths so it didn't hurt as badly. Finally able to breathe easier, she opened the bottle of cough syrup and took several small sips. Washing it down with the rest of the bottled water the storeowner had given her, she closed her eyes again and waited for the medicine to begin to work.

"God, I don't know if you're there, or if you even care, but I need a miracle. I know it's the Christmas season and all, but I'm scared and I don't know what to do anymore." Taking a deep breath, Sara tried to clear her mind and push back the panic that had been prominent for the last several days.

She was in Montana, not California, and David Patterson was nowhere around. She would be successful in finding a place to hide. She just needed to get back on the highway. Opening her eyes, she started to sit up; only to sink back down again as the urge to cough made itself known. Maybe another few minutes wouldn't hurt. She would just sit here and take a small rest. Turning the ignition off, she grabbed a blanket from the backseat and wrapped it around her to keep warm. Leaning her head back against the seat, she allowed her eyes to close as she concentrated on keeping her breathing slow and even.

***

Trent fixed himself a cup of coffee as he waited for the license plate information to appear on his computer. He was hoping to find nothing, but his gut told him that would probably not be the case.

Seeing the message indicator start flashing, he returned to his desk and took a sip of his coffee before clicking the screen open. As the information came up on the screen, he sat up straight and cursed. The car was registered to one David Patterson, who had been attacked two days prior and his car reported stolen. His new bride, Sara Brownell, was wanted for questioning in the attack and theft.

That little gal had attacked a full grown man and stolen his car? Again, his radar was going off. He quickly ran another search on Sara Brownell and wasn't surprised to find that she was squeaky clean. Not even a parking ticket was tied to her name.

On a hunch, he ran her groom's name through the same database. Checking the time, he saw that less than 15 minutes had passed since she had pulled away from the drugstore. She couldn't have gotten far. He wasn't quite sure what was going on, but something in his gut told him it was imperative that he find her and bring her back to town. She needed help and he was the only one in a position to help her at this point.

As the search came back for David Patterson, his fears were confirmed. It wasn't that he had a long record, or even any arrests, but the yellow flag on the account identified him as a person of interest with the feds and that meant there was more to this situation than at first appeared.

Grabbing his coat and hat, he sprinted for the jeep parked out front and headed towards the highway. He didn't even take time to tell Becky, his secretary, goodbye. Sara was in trouble and although he couldn't sanction her having stolen a car, he wanted to be the one to bring her in and see if he could help her in any way. She didn't seem like a criminal to him, but it was his duty to enforce the law. He would find her, and then make a few phone calls and see what other information he could obtain on her groom.

As he neared the entrance to the highway, he spotted her vehicle pulled off to the side of the road. Slowing down, he parked behind the vehicle and noticed that it wasn't running. Cursing again, he climbed out of the jeep and approached the driver's side door. The windows had become fogged up, but he could see her huddled underneath one of the blankets on the front seat.

Not wanting to startle her, but needing to get her attention, he called her name several times, but she didn't seem to hear him. When tapping on the window didn't get her attention either, he tried the door, finding it unlocked. Didn't she have any sense of self-preservation? He definitely needed to have a conversation with her about safety.

Opening the car door, he noticed the car was still warm inside, but Sara didn't stir. Reaching inside, he placed his hand on her head, and then on her neck, looking for a pulse. Her forehead was clammy and even though she was shivering, she was sweating profusely. Her pulse was strong, but as another cough wracked her body, he could see that she was unconscious. Whether by exhaustion or illness, Sara Brownell was a danger to herself as well as others as long as she remained behind the wheel of a car.

Carefully lifting her into his arms, he tucked the blanket around her, carried her to his jeep, and buckled her into the passenger seat. Returning to her vehicle, he grabbed her purse and the small duffel bag from the back seat and then turned on the car's emergency flashers. Sprinting back to the driver's side, he jumped in and headed back to town. Getting on the radio, he contacted Becky, "Get in touch with Dr. Baker and tell him I'm bringing over a young woman. She's been coughing for several days and appears to be running a fever. She's passed out cold. Tell him I'll be at his clinic in 15 minutes."

"Will do. Is there anything else I can do?"

"Yeah, will you get a hold of Jim over at the filling station and have him come tow her car back to town. It's pulled off the road about a mile from the highway entrance. Silver Camry with California plates. I turned the flashers on and the key is under the floor mat."

"I've got it. Where do you want him to tow it?"

"Have him park it over at his place for now. I'll call him later and give him further instructions."

"Okay. Good luck."

Trent looked over at his passenger, still passed out cold and a wave of tenderness passed over him. He didn't know what it was about this woman, but he felt a need to protect her. Seeing her start to stir, he reached over and placed a hand on her shoulder. "Sara, can you hear me?"

Sara felt warmth and for the first time in days, she didn't feel the urge to cough as she took in a slow, deep breath. Her ribs still felt tender, but the agonizing pain was gone. Slowly opening her eyes, she saw that she was in a moving vehicle and immediately tried to sit up as panic assailed her.

"Shush, you're okay. Just sit back and relax. I'm taking you to see Dr. Baker and then we'll get everything else sorted out."

Turning her head to locate the source of the voice, she found herself sinking in the warm gaze of the sheriff, Trent Harding. "Where…" Swallowing, she tried again, "Where am I?"

"I found you parked off the side of the road. You're in my jeep and I'm taking you back to town so Dr. Baker can look at you. You're running a fever and were passed out in your car."

Sara shook her head, "I don't need to see a doctor. I was just resting. I took some of the cough medicine and was waiting for it to start working before I got back on the highway. I didn't want to risk having an accident if I started coughing again."

"Well, I'll feel better after Dr. Baker takes a look. Sara, I ran the plates on the car." Trent paused and watched for her reaction as he made this statement. Instead of guilt or even remorse, he saw immediate fear and panic take over.

Trent had trained at the FBI facility in Quantico for several months prior to returning to his hometown. The bureaucracy of the federal government had been more than he could stomach. He had no doubt in his mind that he would have made a fine profiler and field agent, but Castle Peaks was home, and it suited him just fine.

His training came in useful at times like these, as he evaluated her response to him having checked up on her. Sara was scared, and not because she had stolen her husband's car.

Sara tried to sit up again. She had to convince him to let her go. "The car's not mine. It belongs to my fiancé."

Trent gave her a sideways glance, before saying, "Is your fiancé in the habit of reporting his car stolen when he lets you borrow it?"

David had reported his car stolen. Great! "His car was reported stolen?"

"Yep. And, according to the California Highway Patrol records, someone going by the name of Sara Brownell is the prime suspect. Oh, and she's also wanted for questioning in the attack of David Patterson, the owner of the car."

Sara sank back into the seat. She watched Trent for a minute before asking, "Have you reported in that you found me, yet?"

Trent shook his head, trying to figure out why she was asking. Sara reached out and grabbed his arm, "Please don't. Please don't tell anyone that I'm here. He'll know soon enough because I bought the cough syrup. Please, just take me back to my car and let me go. I didn't steal his car and I can't go back to San Francisco." Sara knew she was begging, but Trent was her only hope. As she finished her plea, another bout of coughing took over and she hugged her ribs, trying to keep the pain from stealing her self-control.

Trent pulled up in front of the medical clinic and turned the jeep off. Turning to look at her, he placed his hand on her back and rubbed slow circles until the coughing fit eased. Talking to himself, he asked, "What are you mixed up in?"

Sara had heard his question, but just shook her head and kept her eyes looking down at her lap. She couldn't go into the details. Who would believe her?

"Let's go see Dr. Baker and then we'll sort the rest of this out."

Thank You

Dear Reader,

Thank you for choosing to read my books out of the thousands that merit reading. I recognize that reading takes time and quietness, so I am grateful that you have designed your lives to allow for this enriching endeavor, whatever the book's title and subject.

Now more than ever before, Amazon reviews and Social Media play vital role in helping individuals make their reading choices. If any of my books have moved you, inspired you, or educated you, please share your reactions with others by posting an Amazon review as well as via email, Facebook, Twitter, Goodreads, -- or even old-fashioned face-to-face conversation! And when you receive my announcement of my new book, please pass it along. Thank you.

For updates about New Releases, as well as exclusive promotions, visit my website and sign up for the VIP mailing list. Click here to get started: www.morrisfenrisbooks.com

I invite you to visit my Facebook page often

facebook.com/AuthorMorrisFenris

where I post not only my news, but announcements of other authors' work.

For my portfolio of books on Amazon, please visit my Author Page:

Amazon USA:
amazon.com/author/morrisfenris

Amazon UK:
https://www.amazon.co.uk/Morris%20Fenris/e/B00FXLWKRC

You can also contact me by email:
authormorrisfenris@gmail.com

With profound gratitude, and with hope for your continued reading pleasure,

Morris Fenris
Author & Publisher

Made in the USA
Columbia, SC
29 October 2020